To Beth

FUNNY LOCATIONS

COLLECTED STORIES

PAUL WARTENBERG

Hope you enjoy these and be safe on I-4!

Paul W.

Copyright ©2023 Paul Wartenberg
All rights reserved.
ISBN-13: 9798871562260
Library of Congress control number:

DEDICATION

Many thanks to everyone with the writing groups I've known:
From Ft. Lauderdale like the Writers Network of South Florida I
joined for a few years when I worked in Broward County, an informal
writing group that met in Land O'Lakes between 2006 through 2013,
the Writers 4 All Seasons group from Polk County when I moved there
in 2013, and the Lakeland Writers group that's part of the Florida
Writers Association.
You've kept me writing and provided solid feedback on a lot of the
stories within this collection. Thank you, and best of luck in getting
your stories to the readers waiting for you

CONTENTS

Road Trip to Vegas	1
...All Others Pay Cash	6
Sunset View	11
Fifth Annual Office Golf Showdown	17
Overdue	26
Snipe Hunt	40
Welcome to Florida	69
Where the Snow Is Gray	79
The Hide and Seek Suitcase	95
That Last Minute Thing	97
Just Throwing This Out There	102
A Wandering Muse	104
My Last Prayer	108
The Librarian	111
The Voynich Key	
The Girl With Angel Wings	133
Author's Notes	139
About the Author	155

ROAD TRIP TO VEGAS

"Road trip to Vegas," says my Dad as though we're going on a grocery run.

"Don't you usually ride with Mac?" I ask as Dad tosses me a travel bag.

"Mac's already flown ahead." He grabs a suitcase he's already packed. "He and Orly are gonna wait for us. It should only take a couple days straight driving to get there."

Funny thing about Dad, having been a Navy pilot for thirty years he doesn't like to fly on planes anymore. He grumbled once about not trusting anybody else in the cockpit.

"No stops on this trip?" I watch Dad get to the SUV in the garage to load his gear. I notice the cooler's already in the back seat.

"Not much to stop for other than gas, food, and sleep." Dad gives me his this-is-serious look. "We could if you need to."

I shrug. "I'm two months into losing my tech job at Canaveral and my resume isn't getting any love. I got nowhere to go and time to waste. Just worried about how you'll handle it."

Dad pats my shoulder. "You know me."

I do. It means he'll do most of the sleeping while I do most of the driving. At least I'll get control of the radio because he'll nap in the back.

The drive itself isn't much, I've done it three times. Just getting on I-95 out of Daytona through Jacksonville, then straight west on I-10 until we run out of Texas, then we have to figure out which highways aren't delayed with construction through New Mexico and Arizona. Easy.

This trip is different. Dad's not napping in the back seat all the way through like he's done before, he's drinking coffee from his thermos and reading some weird diagrams I can't make sense of when I glance back using the rear-view mirror. When we stop for gas outside of Tallahassee I take a moment to look for them but Dad's got them shoved under an armpit for safekeeping.

"I got this round." Dad gets the steering wheel to let me take a turn napping, but he keeps the papers with him, shoving them under my book bag I left in the front passenger seat. I know better than to make a grab for them, but it leaves me worrying and sleepless.

We don't talk much until we reach the edge of Louisiana. "Dad, you know they got casinos in New Orleans," I drop the suggestion while it's mine turn at the steering wheel driving through the early morning darkness.

"True," Dad mutters from under his driving hat he uses to cover his face during sleep. "But you know me and my Navy buddies have a soft spot for Vegas. We'd stop off during our taxi flights between Norfolk and San Diego, play a few nights, share a few laughs. It's how we were back when we were younger."

"Yeah, I know you've got memories," I reply. I give it a few moments before I ask, "You guys aren't going to pull another casino heist, are you?"

"Heh." He lifts his hat from his face as he sits upright in the back seat. His eyes gleam thanks to the semi-truck riding on our bumper reflecting bright lights off the rear-view. "You know full well my flight crew's gotten that out of our system."

I shake my head. "Be honest, you're planning something."

FUNNY LOCATIONS

"It's not a casino heist." Dad leans forward to rest his head on the back of the passenger seat. "I admit the temptation's always there, but *everybody* gets that way. Everyone wants to pull a casino heist their first time to Vegas. You get over it once you try it. You should know yourself."

He pats my shoulder with a laugh. "Admit it. You and those Amish kids on Rumspringa almost pulled yours off. Closest I've ever known anybody to make it out the door with the loot."

That brings up a memory I don't want to rehash, so it shuts me up for most of the drive from there. I keep noticing how Dad shifts between reading those blueprints and his deep naps, the kind where he snores for real, which tells me he's readying himself for serious exertion when we get to our destination.

"So why are you telling me all this?" asks the cashier girl at the Sunoco gas station in Ozona, Texas.

"Because long trips make me narrate everything," I answer while paying for the fill-up. "Gotta talk to somebody. And *somebody* has to bear witness."

Dad stops his naps once we cross the highway along the Grand Canyon. He burns up his smartphone alternating calls between Mac and some other person. As we reach the Strip he tells me, "We've got a room at Caesar's."

"That's a step up."

"Well, no expense too much this trip," Dad replies.

I look over my shoulder. "That's it, isn't it? One of you guys is dying and you're pulling one last heist?"

Dad scowls at me. "Just keep your eye on the road. What have I told you about being reckless?"

"I'm not the one being reckless here." I know Dad's always a major planner, every detail jotted out, which is why those blueprints bother me. Dad's also stubborn enough not to admit what he's doing is dangerous, and he keeps going when most sane men would back down. Ironically that makes him unpredictable, at least to his own son.

Mac and Orly are at the casino driveway waving us in, along with an Elvis impersonator I've never seen before. We unload the SUV and wait for the valets, but it's a busy hotel so the wait's going to be long. Dad's busy with his vet buddies so he sticks me with this new guy, dressed up from the *Blue Hawaii* movie and looking like he was ready to switch to proper "Vegas Elvis" attire. He's about my age, but I know Mac and Orly didn't have sons so I have no idea who's bringing this guy and why. I nod at him. "First time to Vegas?"

He tries smiling the way the King did, but he's got to work on it. He answers in a language I can't recognize, sounding like a mix of Farsi and Klingon. This is what I get for flunking out of college-level German.

The Elvis wannabe hands me his smartphone, glowing in my hand with odd tracking lines that makes me think of neon-lit race cars. He presses his finger on the screen to slide back and forth across a bunch of images that look like flying saucers hovering over key national monuments. I try to nod and smile, but I have no idea why he's got a picture of Cleveland in this batch.

After we get the key cards for the hotel room Dad pulls me to one side with a thick envelope in hand. "Go ahead with your stuff," he whispers.

"Wait." I glance towards his crew. They're already impatient for my father, and they're ready to go on their thing. "Dad, seriously, you shouldn't do this. These heists never work out."

"It's not a heist, and stop worrying." Dad shoves the envelope in my hands. "I got five thousand for you. Just stick to the Blackjack tables and you should do okay."

"Dad, please." The money has me worried, it's the most he's ever loaned me. I raise one hand to his shoulder to pull him close to whisper. "You're going crazy this time. This new guy bothers me. You're teaming up with an Elvis impersonator with language issues and a poor eye for photography."

"Relax." Dad hugs me before he steps away, a knowing smile on his face. "He's been vouched. It's cool."

FUNNY LOCATIONS

And that was two days ago. I've played the tables, won some money. Everybody's got a system, I know. But mine works, even with the floor manager glaring at me like I'm a card counter. Relax boss, I'm solid. I've only gotten the pot from five up to twenty thousand. It's not like I'm breaking the casino one table at a time. Definitely not like that guy they're dragging out right now screaming how *his* plan would have worked. Seriously, bro, you *got caught*. What a noob.

I'm keeping myself to the casino, either the floor to eat and gamble and then the hotel room to shower. But I haven't slept all this time, stressed out on the waiting. It's getting me to where I'm taking more risk. Moving on from Blackjack to something a little more high stakes. The casino boss talks me into this crazy members-only poker game in the penthouse, and I am too tired to argue. Only now at this point in the game I am finally getting a call from the parental figure.

Dad's voice is rushed. "Son, I'm gonna need a little help here."

"I told you the heist wasn't going to work out," I sigh back. "You gonna need bail?"

"Don't need bail. And I told you it wasn't a heist," Dad answers, "but we're going to need some help with this flying saucer we're sneaking out of Area 51. How soon can you get to me out on Highway 93, out towards the Moapa intersection?"

"I'm a little tied up," I reply while glancing around the table I'm at, and all the heavy rollers glaring back at me. "I got roped into a big money poker game with a Yakuza boss nicknamed Zero Cuts and the pot is up to three million now at least."

"Well, get out of it, and hurry." Dad hangs up.

I toss the phone onto the pile of money on the table. "My dad's hijacking a UFO and he needs some help. You in or out?"

The Yakuza boss across the table from me gives it some serious thought, tapping all ten fingers on the suede surface. "I'm in," Zero Cuts smiles with leonine interest. "But make your play."

"Fine." I push my total stack of chips into the middle of the table. "I call. Now let's go rescue Dad."

...ALL OTHERS PAY CASH

This really, really happened. I'm serious.

Let me say first that I hate taxes. Well, not the actual paying of taxes. I mean, I do try to uphold my civic duties and I believe firmly that my tax dollars are going to needed public services.

What I hate are the damn forms.

I'm a librarian. That means every new year, the IRS sends boxes and boxes of every conceivable form people need for filing their taxes. The basic 1040 forms with the itemized deduction sheets, forms for mortgages and investments and stock options and overseas holdings and travel expenses and child support and other things that people seem to do that have to be taxed. Every library out there gets thousands upon thousands of tax forms, regardless if the locals need them or not (being in an urban community, I don't think I've ever had a farmer come in for Schedule F forms).

Along with the thousands of forms, I get thousands of people looking for those forms. It's that they don't even know which form they need that drives me batty. "Oh, I need a form to deduct my accounts." "Oh, your IRA accounts, or other investments?" "No, wait,

FUNNY LOCATIONS

maybe I need an expense deduction..." "Okay, what kind of expenses?" "No, wait..."

At that point, I hide under the table until the person leaves or is crushed by a falling bus, whichever comes first.

Remember when that Forbes guy ran for president on a flat tax platform? It wasn't the tax reduction I supported: it was the brilliant idea of having it all on one little postcard. Whew. No more forms. Sic Semper Papyrus.

I guess that's not too funny. Probably have too many forms of your own to fill out and agonize over. But you see, pretty much from January to April, that's all people want from me. Business people, caregivers, college students, retirees, other librarians, you name it. They all come to me.

That was probably why an angel stood before my desk with the question, "Do you have the form for moving expenses?"

See, you started laughing. Maybe not a laugh, but certainly a prolonged giggle.

The angel was tall and slender, broad wings cresting above the shoulders before curving down toward the ankles. There was no halo, but I guess the small golden crown pressing down on the unkempt hair could have been mistaken for one by other observers.

"Moving expenses?" I asked, puzzled.

"Yeah." The angel's wings shrugged. "Tax forms, I need tax forms."

I stared at the angel with impressive awe. "Wow. The IRS has really extended their reach this year..."

"I see you have forms on display for regular filings, but I need one for moving expenses."

"All right." I glanced through the display area looking for Form 3903—Moving Expenses. It took me a moment to consider the next question. "Uh, where might you be moving from?"

"Philadelphia."

"Oh." I spotted an empty spot in the display area. "Seems everybody else got those forms."

7

"That would happen, wouldn't it?"

"Relax. We keep here in this notebook of reproducible forms. In case we run out of the original sheets."

"Well, thank God for that."

I opened the notebook to the page and released the sheet from its binder. "You'll have to make a copy of it and bring it back."

The angel glanced at the sheet, then back at me. "Ah..."

"Don't worry. The IRS sent us the reproducible, so they'll accept a copy of it."

"It's not that, it's..." The angel appeared sheepish.

I pointed to the far corner. "The photocopiers are over there. Ten cents a page."

The angel stared toward the copier sign, a worrisome frown signaling more embarrassment. "I, um, don't have any change."

"Excuse me?"

"Well, you don't see any pockets on this robe, do you?"

"The copiers can take dollar bills, you know . . ."

"I'm an angel. I don't have any money."

"Well then, what the hell do you need a tax form . . . Oh, sorry," I grimaced over my blunder.

"You can curse. Just don't take you-know-who's name in vain, all right?"

"Didn't you just did?"

"No, I did indeed thank God that there was a reproducible available. Check the fine print."

"Well, why do you need tax forms if you don't have any money?"

The angel shrugged. Either that or the wings needed a scratch. "You probably know angels spend a lot of time going everywhere performing miracles."

"Sure."

"Sometimes the assignment goes long-term. Not some show-up-heal-a-guy-amen thing you can do in three minutes, but one of those prolonged Gee-father-and-son-need-to-reconcile-before-mom-dies-in-terrible-bus-accident melodramas that take a whole month."

FUNNY LOCATIONS

I nodded in understanding.

"During those assignments you take human form, get a job, pay the rent, avoid romantic attachments, the usual."

"Oh, so when you get a job...

"Right. The minute you get a paycheck, the IRS rides you like a Harley." The angel shuddered, considering some blighted thought. "Do you know what it's like to get audited? Having Mammon pluck off your feathers is a more pleasurable experience."

"That explains the need to fill out the forms. But where's the money you earned?"

"I give it away upon completion of said assignment." The angel nodded. "I'm an angel. Pure habit."

"What if you owe back taxes?"

"Never happened." The angel knocked on wood. "I've always worked it out so I get a refund. And those checks usually go to the orphans, bless 'em..."

"Yeah, but... You're an angel. Perform some miracle. Make the copier work for free or something."

The angel shook his head. "Union rules. No miracles for personal gain."

I sighed. "Well, you're an angel. I think I can trust you with this, so... Maybe you can take it up to heaven and have someone up there copy the form...

"Maybe not. Somebody else here might need it, and time has no meaning there. It might be years before I get back . . ."

"Argh." I reached into my pocket and found my wallet. I yanked a dollar bill out and handed it over. "Here. You can accept alms. Distribute the change when you're done."

The angel smiled a heavenly sign of contentment and hope. "Bless you. You will be praised in heaven for this..."

"Really? Can you go down to that Pentecostal church then and tell those guys? They've been damning me for years for having 'Romeo and Juliet' on the shelves..."

"Deal."

It didn't turn out so simple, though. The angel came back a minute later with the change. "You can have this back."

"Oh. You're not going to distribute this among the poor?"

"It's not that. I won't be able to speak to the Pentecostals on your behalf. While I thank you for letting me use the copier, I can't really accept you buying any favors from a heavenly agent. Some people can construe this as an indulgence."

"What?"

"True. Even with a dollar."

I sighed. "Look, go make the copy and bring me back the change. I'll put the change in a charity box, and I won't ask you to speak to the Pentecostals. Okay?"

"Okay." The angel turned to go.

"Hey! Wait a second."

"Yes."

"Is there . . ." I leaned forward to whisper. "Isn't there something your boss can do? About getting rid of these damnable tax forms?"

The angel actually considered it for a minute. "No. If the Lord Our God had anything to say about this, do you think I'd be filling these out?"

"Good point..."

"Of course. This is the IRS we're talking about." The angel bowed in all seriousness before departing.

And this happened. It really did. So what if the wings said "St. Peters Pizza—We Deliver"? It could have been marketing for one of those part-time jobs angels still get from time to time...

SUNSET VIEW

Steve Fowler leaned back in his lounger, listening to the soft distant whooshing of the waves rolling onto the beach, noting the color changes of the sunset sky against cotton-weave clouds above him. Near the porch, his German Shepherd Badger barked loudly and danced wildly facing the shrubs, noticeably finding that turtle from yesterday still desperately hiding. The whiskey glass in his hand was mostly full, dinnertime was still in the planning stage, his neighbors all across Sunset Key were walking in from the shore, and he was certain his favorite episode of *Law & Order* was going to be on A&E in thirty minutes.

Steve's first sigh indicated his contentment with life. His second sigh was responding to the soft footfalls coming up the porch ramp behind him.

"Chamayra," Steve called out, "I'm not letting you take my boat."

"Damn." The voice was soft, smooth. The young woman circled the lounger to greet him, a disappointed scowl otherwise marring a young pretty face. "You always know. I wasn't even wearing shoes this time and still you knew."

Steve smiled and pointed to his dog. "Badger didn't take away his attention from that turtle he found. He doesn't like strangers. He likes you."

"And it's pretty rude to automatically assume I'm here for your boat."

"Well, you're always here asking to borrow my boat."

Chamayra smiled. "You could ask me if I'm here for dinner."

Steve smiled back, chuckling for a moment. "Are you here for my boat?"

The woman rolled her eyes, gasping in exasperation. "C'mon, don't you know me well enough to trust me with your boat?"

"Where are you going to take it?" Steve took a sip from his whiskey glass.

"Just across the way to Anclote Key," Chamayra answered. "And I'll be upfront with you, I'm taking a few friends."

Steve rolled his eyes in response. "Okay, for starters Anclote's pretty much fifty feet away from this shoreline, you can wade across the inlet and not get your arms wet."

"Steve." The woman crossed her arms.

"Secondly, I've got this sneaking feeling your friends are from Miami."

"No, they're not."

"What are their names?"

Chamayra paused.

"Let me guess, one of them is Juan."

"No." She looked away. "He's in jail for illegal firearm possession. The guys asking for the boat are from Ybor."

Steve arched an eyebrow. "A new crew of revolutionary wanna-bes?"

"They are not revolutionaries." Chamayra kept her arms crossed, but her eyes flashed a deeper anger. "I mean that we aren't."

"You're no soldier."

"No, I'm not."

"But you want to take it to Cuba."

"Yours is the only boat I know that can make the trip to Key West and from there to the Cuban coast. Steve, we're going in to get family members."

"It's still Cuba." Steve sighed. "There are about twenty things that can go wrong if you go."

Chamayra knelt down, letting one arm to lean against the porch floor. "And there's one thing right. And you know it."

He pursed his lips, thinking, then took another sip of whiskey.

Chamayra stood, growling. "Steve, it's not like you use it that often, anyway."

"I use my boat often enough. I do get the occasional fishing party. Anyway, I'm not worried about me. I'm worried about you. You are way too obsessed about this."

"I've got my reasons." Chamayra got defensive about that, and Steve nodded. He'd known Chamayra long enough, much like everyone else on this island knew everyone else.

"Steve, please." Chamayra stepped away, taking a seat on the porch railing facing him. Badger finally approached to give her a friendly sniff, hopping up eagerly licking at her arms and face. "Please, you can trust me."

"Okay, I'll trust you."

She smiled at that.

"Not with the boat."

The smile faded.

"I can trust you with the truth."

Her scowled shifted slightly from anger to confusion. "What truth?"

Steve placed his whiskey glass on the patio table next to him. "Why I don't want you getting mixed up in Cuba business. Because I got mixed up in Cuba business."

The reply was half-shock, half-giggle. "What?!"

Steve closed his eyes. "Don't tell anyone else. I'm CIA. Retired."

Chamayra paused, thinking for a full minute. "Hell no. You're barely 35, you're too young to be retired. Even with the CIA, which sounds so wrong about you."

Steve leaned back, opened his eyes, gave her the full stare. "I was 20 years old in 1992. My dad was Navy Intel, my mom a certified accountant for a Houston oil firm. I was a prominent member of the Young Republicans at Florida State. The government trusted me for an assignment, deep cover, quick training and insertion."

"Into Cuba?"

"Think about the year. Bush was running for re-election. The Gulf War was fading into memory and he needed something big to wow the voters. Overthrow Castro, be the President in office when Cuba was freed after 30 years of Communist rule, make himself look like a can-do go-to guy."

"So what happened?"

"It was me and three other guys. We didn't have much background in military, but Langley officials felt after three decades of intelligence fiascoes, they couldn't trust security with the guys already working in the Anti-Castro militias. So they went with rookies. Us. We knew the language, all four of us already had extensive field experience, and we were eager to go for God and Country."

"Field experience?" she groaned. "As a Young Republican? Doing what, canvassing houses for votes?"

"I did stuff. Very classified. Anyway, about Cuba," Steve took another sip of whiskey. "Whole thing went to hell within a day. Supplies were stolen by Cali smugglers. Our contact inland turned out to be an ex-Bulgarian who couldn't speak any Spanish, or English for that matter. Only there for the girls, the perv. And then things got really screwy."

Steve paused, long enough for Chamayra to blurt, "Well, dammit, keep going!"

"We stuck to our deep cover IDs but, well, something snapped. In us." Steve sipped some more whiskey. "Honus completely bought into his fake persona of an up-and-coming baseball pitcher. Tried out for the national team, completely believing his name was... is Esteban Diaz Argello. Actually played well for the team at the Sydney Olympics. He did eventually make it back across the strait, working bullpen for the Expos now. Got a 4.32 ERA and 9 saves this year. Ought to get a better contract from the Yankees next year."

He sighed, then continued. "Mark married a farmer's daughter, wanting to settle down, worked the sugar canes last I saw him. I heard two years ago he went a little more loopy, thinking he's French. The last guy, David, couldn't handle it as a taxi driver, went to Havana and made an attempt on Fidel Castro's third cousin Benny."

"Hey, at least he tried to follow through on the mission," Chamayra offered.

Steve arched an eyebrow. "With two coconuts and a paper mâché sword?"

"Well, what happened to you?"

"When I saw the whole thing was heading for the crapper, I escaped. Wandered cross-country for two years, working my way to Gitmo. I made it, avoided capture. Thank God the security forces never suspect an Elvis Impersonator."

"WHAT?!" Chamayra slid off the railing, barely landing on her feet.

"It was the only way I could survive." Steve shrugged. "Back then, I looked a lot like Elvis did in 'Blue Hawaii.' Lip-synced to a scratched-up record, signed a few autographs, made a cameo appearance in a really cheesy Norwegian Z-movie some artist was filming for school, then I surfed across Guantanamo Bay into the Marine base. Had to lip-sync to a few more CDs before I was debriefed, though."

Chamayra took a moment, then laughed uncontrollably. She leaned so far forward that Badger could reach her face and lick her nose, making it harder for her to stop.

Steve looked away for a moment, admiring the view of the sunset sinking further into the gulf. Finally, he sighed and added. "Go to my billiards table. Look on the right wall. Third row up, fourth across to the right."

Chamayra stopped laughing. Standing up, she scowled quizzically at Steve before opening the door into his home. Badger followed her in, and Steve listened to her footsteps.

"Here?" she finally shouted. A minute later, she added, "I don't see anything!"

"Do you see that photo of the marlin dangling off a pier? Look over to its right by one, that's it. That photo on the right."

"Okay." Another long pause. "That's you?"

Steve smirked. "Yes. I looked pretty good in that Elvis getup, didn't I?"

Another long pause. "Hmm. What's this picture of you next to that? I can tell it's you as a kid, but what's a kid that age shaking hands with Casper Weinberger?"

"Oh, that." Steve answered. "Well, if I didn't tell the Senate subcommittee I'm certainly not telling you."

Chamayra laughed at that, a short gentle giggle. "No, you're gonna need to tell me."

Badger paced back through the door onto the porch, sitting down facing Steve with a slight tilt to his head.

Steve sighed, figuring he'd probably missed his television show. Still, there was dinner to plan, and he thought smiling to himself of the recipe that served best for two.

FIFTH ANNUAL OFFICE GOLF SHOWDOWN

"Hello, again, welcome back, for those of you just joining us, this is the Fifth Annual Office Golf Showdown being held this year at beautiful downtown SouthTrust Bank. I'm David Anderson, with me as always is Peter Smith..."

"Not yet, Dave, I haven't finished my cup of coffee yet."

"Can't help it, the cameras are back on. We're getting towards the end of this tourney, and we're working our way up from the 17th floor to the 18th. This is going to be one of the trickier greens to be played here, as it'll start right next to the photocopier in the hallway outside of the 3YK subsidiary offices, through the fire exit in what has got to be the toughest leg of this hole, going up onto the 18th and through the open secretarial floor there, before reaching the putting cup placed behind the trash bin next to the desk of the CFO of the Genu-Flex wholesalers division in office 1846."

"In real golf, of course, this would be a Par 6. For these players, sadly, I'd go with a Par 23, just to be fair and all."

"Now, Peter, you're being harsh. We've got some of the best office golf players in the tri-county area playing here today, and we've already seen some incredible action already."

"Yes, I would have to agree, pity about that fax machine though."

"Teeing up right now is Frank Delcoy, who made that marvelous shot earlier through the 12th floor filing cabinets, and he's going to his driver here to make the shot."

"Seeing as how he's got to make it up that stairwell, he's going to need all the power he's got. Gravity is not his friend here."

"Frank does indeed have to work for this shot. As we've seen earlier on the fifth hole, he doesn't have enough strength in his swing to make long drives."

"He did, however, more than compensate for that with that lucky bounce off the intern's head."

"The crowd is quieting. He's in his stance. Here's the swing... and... Oh my God, he shanked it!"

"Incoming!"

"AAAUUGGH!"

"Where is it? There! It's bouncing out past the shredder."

"Are you okay?"

"I'm fine. My reflexes are still rather good, thank you very much."

"Our cameraman's a little shaken, the ball came *this close* to taking off his ear. I think he's still traumatized by that hit he took during our coverage of the Chrysler Building Open."

"Get over it, Mikey. You're still alive."

"I have to tell you, that was not a good shot."

"Major understatement, Dave. The ball just went completely to the right off Delcoy's swing, causing disruption over in this direction, knocking over what appears to be a statue of a weeping... a weeping... well, it was a swan-shaped thing, and just shot over into the office manager's cubicle where... can we get confirmation on this?"

"Yes, we can. Our cameras are zooming in right now, Peter. Yes! The coffee mug he was holding was completely obliterated!"

"Along with next month's spreadsheet projections covering his desk."

"Essentially, poor Frank here has played into the rough as it were,

FUNNY LOCATIONS

getting into a part of the floor the tourney administrators were hoping to avoid. Shag carpeting. Nasty playing surface for golf."

"True. I've lost entire buckets of practice shots in my wife's living room."

"Delcoy is not happy. He's taking a moment to berate his caddie, Jackson from Accounting, and now he's... oh, he's taking out his frustration on the golf club!"

"Not to mention the linoleum floor."

"It's sad when we witness a meltdown like this, Peter. A player of his caliber shouldn't give in to his anxieties and frustrations. At least not in public."

"I can't agree with you on that one, David. It's great for us because we get to make commentary on this later during the hour-long sports news reports for the next week or so."

"Still, here comes building security to escort Delcoy from the building."

"Think they'll use pepper spray this time?"

"No bet. The cans are already in their hands."

"And... there he goes. We can put him down for 'Did Not Complete.'"

"Well. There's that for excitement. Next up is Greg McDashett, coming over from the AutoNation offices, where he'd recently won that building's rather exciting and challenging tourney."

"He comes in with an excellent control of his shot, David. He uses just enough power to get his drives to go long, yet has enough finesse to control where the ball will be landing."

"He's not taking any time to warm up here. Amazing that he's not taking a moment to measure out his shot."

"Greg is looking to finish early, Dave, most likely so he won't get stuck in traffic this afternoon."

"Well, we'll just have to see if this affects his drive here. He's ready to swing. And... gets a good placement, that ball is sailing long and straight for the fire exit..."

"He's already got a good start here, let's see how he works on the ricochet to get it upstairs..."

"Hits the fire extinguisher!"

"It's got a good angle upward! He clears the guard railing!"

"A good bounce into the hallway on 18th! What a shot!"

"Ah, yes, leave it to a Scotsman to show you how it's done!"

"And the crowd applauds good and long here, Peter. Well deserved!"

"Excellent shot, David. Excellent. Give me a minute. Got to finish my coffee."

"Well, while my compatriot ducks out of the camera view for a moment, let me mention that the next player coming up has now got to make a hell of a good drive here to keep within one of Greg McDashett, the current leader on the board. With Delcoy disqualified, we've got a two-man, uh, two-person tournament now, with McDashett at 3 under and Sarah Williams, who's been playing well on her home turf here in the SouthTrust building. Williams, best known for her work in the Investments department of the bank corporation as well as her wicked shot ricochet to win last year's qualifying round, has an advantage in knowing how to make these shots in this type of building, but does have some concerns regarding her ability to drive long off her tees."

"Okay, I'm back David. Did I miss anything?"

"I was discussing Williams' problems with driving long off her tee shot."

"Oh, that. It has to do with the way she turns her hips. She's very conscious of her hips."

"The men among the crowd with their wolf whistling when she sets up can't help her in that regard."

"Yes, that is a pity isn't it? I can hope someday that we would be civilized enough to appreciate women for their truest finest attributes."

"You can't impress her, Peter. She's engaged already."

"Well, that's a damn bloody shame isn't it?"

FUNNY LOCATIONS

"Here we go. She's getting into the swing now..."

"Here comes the wolf whistles."

"There goes her shot!"

"Gets a low slice... no, gets a good ricochet off the plastic palm tree and through the fire exit door."

"Misses the fire extinguisher though, but gets a good bounce over the guardrail on this end of the floor and over the open space onto the top of the stairwell."

"Ooo, look out it's rolling back."

"Not good. Needs to slow down or else it'll bounce down the stairs."

"The last thing she needs is to play against a high narrow step."

"And... there. Just on the edge."

"Lucky break for her. Williams has some ground to make up however, especially with McDashett positioned already in the 18th floor hallway."

"Williams takes the walk up the stairs while McDashett takes the elevator. With her the farthest shot, Sarah has got to work her way onto the 18th."

"Time for a commercial break, then."

"Sadly, no. The toll-free operators are on strike this week, so we lost the advertising from the 1997 Greatest Dance Hits retailers."

"Didn't we get any sponsorships for this?"

"We had. Enron."

"...Oh."

"Well, Williams is ready for her shot into the hallway. I seriously doubt she can make it that far to the green, Peter."

"She has worked some good angle shots before, David. Can't rule her out yet."

"Gets a five-iron from her caddie Joy from Atrium Cafeteria. Measures her shot out."

"Five-iron might not work here."

"What would work here?"

"Four-iron and a well-placed intern for extra bounce."

"Not her call here. She takes position, gets up a good swing . . . whoa! Gets a good curve just through the doorway and into the hall."

"Better yet, she gets a great bounce off of that faux Degas painting and has her shot making it well past the secretaries' desks, and... well, look at that!"

"An excellent roll! She gets her ball into the GenuFlex office!"

"She's incredibly close to the green now, David! And she didn't have to use an intern to make it! I'm impressed!"

"McDashett has just gotten off the elevator in time to see that shot, and look at how he's shaking his head."

"I don't think he's stunned by the shot. He's worried he can't use that Degas painting to make a good ricochet."

"How much did you think that painting cost, Peter?"

"A dime, and that for the frame. I said it was a fake."

"How can you be sure?"

"The original's in *my* hallway."

"Good point. So replacing it shouldn't cost too much."

"Agreed. Here's McDashett now working on his shot."

"Going with that four-iron, so he's probably looking for an intern to bounce it off of."

"Don't talk so loud, Dave. Half the office just dived for cover."

"Here's his swing, and . . . Oh no! Slice!"

"Into the wrong office!"

"Whose office is that?"

"Let's check the directory. Hmm, that room is... uh oh."

"What? Greg's boss?!"

"No, wrong building. It's worse, his father-in-law."

"His father-in-law works here?!"

"Why do you think he works over in AutoNation?"

"Here he comes. With an inappropriately placed coffee stain."

"This is not good."

"How can you tell?"

"Well, when someone starts off yelling with words like 'lawyers' and 'unemployment,' that's never good."

FUNNY LOCATIONS

"As the audience can probably hear in the background, we're currently paused for an emergency tongue-lashing from a high-level SouthTrust executive. Apparently, Greg McDashett's father-in-law does not believe nor does he support the athletic endeavor that is office golf. He is most certainly in the mood to kick us out of the building. And from the sounds of it, from the rooftop."

"Well, we're just going to wait and see at what moment he realizes the bank is getting $20 million from our cable company for broadcasting rights."

Long awkward pause.

"And... he's letting McDashett play through!"

"I've got mixed feelings about this, David. While it's beautiful that we'll be able to finish today's tourney, it's a pity that Greg there has to take what could very well be the toughest shot of the day."

"It's not that tough."

"It will be when you've got to start worrying about the upcoming family dinner this Thanksgiving."

"McDashett is going in to that office now to make his shot. He's tied now with Williams for the lead, and he's got to make a good one here to make it onto the green."

"Can we get a camera crew in there now to view the shot?"

"Harry is getting in there now with the SteadiCam and... Okay, move out of the way, Harry."

"Good boy. Mustn't put the SteadiCam in harm's way."

"McDashett leans forward to get a good angle to the ball... swings back... good focused swing-through... gets it back out into the secretaries' floor space and... there we go!"

"Finally found that intern to bounce it off of!"

"Bonus points?"

"No. The intern's still standing."

"The ball heads right into the GenuFlex office, makes a wicked ricochet off a potted plant, and rolls gently... yes, it's rolling right up to the green placemat carpet! What a shot!"

"He's recovered nicely here, David! And his father-in-law is now suitably impressed!"

"He's getting his putter now from his caddie as he walks his way into the office and up to the line-up shot for the Office Max putting cup!"

"The Office Max putting cup, brought to you by... oh, wait, we can't do any product placement. Bloody lack of sponsors. Sheesh. Well, apologies."

"Oh, relax. They'll probably just dock your paycheck. Now, he's getting ready to make the shot. What do you think he's going to do here, Peter?"

"I think he's going to hit the ball into the hole, Dave."

"He's taking a moment to measure his swing, looking for the right stance and the right follow-through on the putt."

"He's just got to gently push that ball forward. Easy shot."

"Don't say that. You'll jinx him."

"Too late. I said it."

"Argh. Stop him! He has to know he's been jinxed! Greg! Don't take the shot yet! Wait!"

"He can't hear you from there! It's too late! He's done for!"

"No! I had money on him!"

"There's his swing. He's making the putt and... there! It bounced off that little plastic yellow flag and to the other side of the trash bin!"

"Dammit. You did that on purpose."

"No. Anyway, you can't prove it in court, and I'm sticking to my story."

"...So, he takes the extra swing on the putt to get it back to line up his shot again, and takes a quick swing for the putt and gets it in. Finally. But now he's two down on Sarah Williams, who now takes her time to make her shot onto the green."

"She has to be totally relaxed here to do well. She ought to try for the cup with this shot and avoid a playoff situation."

"Are you jinxing her too?"

"Absolutely not."

FUNNY LOCATIONS

"So you bet on her then?"

"...No. I had money on Shelly from Home Loans. I can't believe she flubbed the entire fourth floor."

"Williams is now getting into her swing . . . look at how she's turning her hips to get an angle shot from the far filing cabinet!"

"I'm looking, I'm seeing!"

"There she goes, just enough power on the swing to hop it... onto the filing cabinet and then off the miniature bust of Jack Welch and onto the desk just above the putting cup!"

"She's getting a great roll off the Collective Bargaining paperwork!"

"And... she makes the shot! My God!"

"Incredible!"

"She gets it to rebound off the stapler and it plops right into the cup!"

"I can't believe it!"

"Stunning!"

"I concur, she looks great in that dress."

"Well, there's going to be some rioting in the Investments offices this afternoon!"

"Oh, I hope not, the last thing we need are out-of-control investors..."

OVERDUE

Rocky Mount, NC
Two Days Ago

They observed David Argussen, his backpack dangling over a faded blue denim jacket, walking towards the downtown parking garage, completely unrecognizable among the hundreds of others upon those very streets. To most, he seemed normal, average, albeit happier than most.

Those who knew better would identify him as the most dangerous library patron alive.

Argussen had been barred from nearly every state university in California. He had been seen in the Santa Fe, New Mexico main branch just prior to the disappearance of their entire Russian literature section. He had been tracked under an alias through Nebraska, Missouri, and Kentucky, with rumors of chaos and empty shelves in his wake. Argussen was a chronic Bibliomaniac, the worst in ninety years, and he was walking away rather briskly from the Braswell Library.

FUNNY LOCATIONS

One of the observers spoke to another. "He's smiling. Definitely has something."

"Someone should tell the trackers with the ALA that he's pretty far from the southwest Georgia hideaway he's supposed to be at." The second observer turned away, grabbing at a satchel. "Let's do it."

Argussen entered the shade of the parking garage with few cares, having secured what he sought ever since his arrival. It took three days to note the weaknesses in that library's security, finding the best moment to liberate perhaps his greatest trophy yet. He had every reason to think this would be his most relaxing and prosperous...

And then he stopped. He sensed... something wrong. Not that anyone had followed him from the library, but still...

The blow came from his left, but he was aware enough to pull away, the fist glancing off of his shoulder. Argussen turned, swinging the backpack onto the concrete ground. He stood in a classic Kenpo defensive stance: Argussen, like many other Bibliomaniacs, knew where to steal the martial arts books.

He faced a dark-clothed figure, shorter and slimmer of build, also in a stance suggestive of the Ninjutsu art. "I don't believe it," he chuckled, "the library has ninjas for security?"

"Not exactly." The voice came from his right. He turned to face a taller, broad-shouldered man in a dark trench coat. In his hands was the rare early print of Dumas' *Le Comte de Monte-Cristo* that Argussen thought was secretly hidden in the back lining of his denim jacket.

"We're not with the local libraries," continued the trench coat man. "We're here to send a message."

Argussen suddenly realized he had turned his back on a ninja. He tried to turn around, but the blow to a sensitive spot between the neck and shoulder came quick. His last thought was if this had anything to do with the Swedish translation of *Jane Eyre* he plundered from the Broken Arrow Library outside of Tulsa.

Gainesville, FL

Seven Weeks Ago

"So this is where he ended up," the woman noted as she passed through the doorway, large oak doors opening into the high-ceiling foyer of the eastern wing of the Smathers Library. "I thought he'd be off looking for that book of his."

The man holding the door for her allowed two college students to pass, then followed inside. "He's actually bounced around through a lot of library systems over the years. This place, at least, has been where he's stayed the longest."

After asking directions at the desk inside a study hall on that floor, the pair headed for a small service elevator in the back. A ride up to the second floor led them to thick glass doors into long ornate hallway, facing south into the Special Collections wing. They entered a high-ceiling room, with two rows of reading tables in the center, and an information desk currently unmanned near a set of doorways.

A shadowy figure stood behind a frosted glass door at the other end of the room. The door opened, revealing a man of average height yet broad-shouldered, with neatly trimmed auburn hair and dark blue eyes blinking warily behind wire-rimmed glasses. "Do you have an appointment?"

"No." The man spoke while his female companion stepped toward the table. "I know full well that you don't give appointments for what we seek, Warren Stern."

Warren glared at the visitor. His shoulders seemed to spread out, his body in a defensive posture. He walked to the information desk and placed a pile of papers atop it. "I'm not for hire anymore. I've got a job now, I've had it for two years and I'm not about to screw this one up."

"You've had a job, didn't you, with the Library of Congress?" The woman spoke, placing her briefcase on the table. "I heard. A bright, promising archivist at the most prominent facility in the world? The only thing I haven't heard is what happened to have them fire you."

Warren nearly snarled at her, paused, then glanced away. "I resigned, actually. That place is almost like another country to me now. And there's nothing I can do, there's nothing you can offer, to assure that I could ever go back there."

He turned. "At least I have a special collection here to take care of. I'm not going to jeopardize this."

"We need your help," the man spoke.

"No." Warren headed for the door back to his office.

"We're losing our collections at our libraries." The man stepped closer to his female compatriot. "We all are. Every system is."

"Yes, I know. Even here at the university." Warren stopped, glancing over his shoulder at them. "Leave it to your circulation departments. That's not my field of expertise."

"No, we don't want to, not anymore," the woman noted, opening the briefcase and pulling out a faint red folder. She tossed the folder to Warren's end of the table. "And what we want is in your field of expertise."

Warren arched an eyebrow, then opened the folder.

Richmond, VA
Yesterday

The small house sat hidden behind a row of shrubs and under the blanket of tall oak trees. The window curtains were all drawn shut, the doors all locked, save for the kitchen entrance in the back where the occupant had his Chinese food delivered. The exterior was well-maintained, had just received a new coat of egg white paint in fact, but somehow seemed void of any life, any presence.

Two figures moved quietly, placing themselves behind an oak tree away from the house. Both were robed in dark fatigues, one noticeably shorter than the other. The short one held a long, cloth-wrapped object while the taller figure opened a satchel dropped at their feet.

"I hate this," the short one snarled in a hushed tone. "Broad daylight, not much cover. He'll see us coming."

"Yoder left twenty minutes ago. There's no sign of surveillance. We're going in on a simple recon, check what he has." The tall one took a thin hand-sized leather notebook from the satchel. "We need to ascertain how many books we're going to be recovering before we re-secure the materials."

The tall one tapped the wrapped object. "And leave the sword."

The short one growled but placed it between the satchel's grips.

The pair approached a side door to the garage. The tall one unzipped the notebook and revealed a set of small thin metal tools. Selecting two, he knelt before the doorknob, gently working both rods into the lock. In five seconds, the lock clicked.

They entered the garage, empty save for the oil stain gathering where a car usually sat. They hurried over to the doorway leading into the house itself, and finding it unlocked they entered into a long hallway.

The hallway was dark, the light switch failing to work. "No light," whispered the tall figure. "This... is odd."

They walked further, slowly, into the house. The hallway led into the foyer area, with a darkened room barely discernible in the shadows.

"Find a light yet?" The short one didn't think to whisper at this point. She glanced around, unable to see a switch.

There was no answer, until a thin beam of light broke into the shadows. The tall one held a pencil flashlight, pointing it in various directions until spotting a light switch on a nearby wall. He flipped the toggle upward. "Yes."

The foyer brightened, enough to see into the adjoining living room. The pair noted one weather-beaten sofa, behind which sat column after column of bookshelves.

The shelves were all empty.

The tall one stepped forward, but then quickly stepped away from the living room. "He knew. It's..."

FUNNY LOCATIONS

There was no need to finish that thought. The tall one turned and quickly ran back down the hallway, pausing only briefly to note the hissing sound usually made by a fuse that was working its way behind one of the walls. He turned the corner, reaching the garage just as he felt the heat increase upon his back. Refusing to turn and watch the house ignite, he slammed his way through the unlocked door and rolled upon the ground, only then witnessing the flames erupting straight through the roof.

The short one took a more traditional route out of an exploding house, and jumped painfully through the nearest wooden plank that had boarded up the foyer window. Feeling the cuts from the splinters and shards of windowpane, she rolled upon the ground as well, doing what she could to get far enough away from the detonation.

She pulled away her black mask, revealing the face of a young Asian woman, dark hair secured in place by a long ponytail. She stood, slowly, feeling the ache of the various cuts along her forearms and legs. She noted none were deep, but refused to take comfort in that.

She stumbled in the direction of the other side of the house, moving away with each step from the increasing heat of the growing inferno. She watched as her partner stepped toward her, carrying the sword and satchel with him. He handed her the covered sword, then pulled off his mask to reveal his unkempt dark hair, trimmed beard, and dark scowling eyes.

"A trap," he snarled. "Yoder knew. Word about Argussen must have spread quicker than planned."

"This shouldn't have been a surprise," the woman answered.

"Now, no." He shook his head. "Stern was wrong. I was wrong. We thought... when they knew what we were doing... they would be afraid."

He watched the flames engulf the house. "They're not. They're going to fight back."

"Good," the woman nodded. "We're taking it seriously, they're taking it seriously. Better this than chasing down scared cattle."

She unwrapped the cloth in her hands, revealing a finely crafted sheath for a samurai's sword. "And from now on, I'm keeping this with me."

Spokane, WA
Five Weeks Ago

Chiyoko Jackson sighed, bored out of her mind, waving her laser gun over another barcode for yet another battered looking book pocket. There sat a pile of torn, shredded book pockets in front of her, and a larger pile of them that she hadn't even gotten to yet.

Work in the circulation department of Gonzaga's Foley Center consisted, at least for her: Finding out titles were no longer on their shelves; finding the pockets of books torn out and left stuffed in the trash bins throughout each of the library's four floors; finding misplaced books from the literature collection shoved haphazardly into the business management collection; and finding herself going slowly insane after three years of weeping for titles no longer within reach.

Chiyoko watched the computer as the pocket's barcode registered within the system, then typed a few keys to list the book as 'Long Gone.' Then she sighed again and picked up the next pocket.

"I take it all your copies of *Swedish Management Styles For Successful Capitalism* are long gone too, huh?"

She turned and smiled, recognizing the voice almost immediately. "Stern! You snuck up on me! Me! Good, you've learned your stealth techniques..."

They hugged briefly, Chiyoko standing up to place both arms around her friend. Warren patted her gently on the back, noting her work pile on the table. "I'm a little surprised to find you're still here."

"Yeah. My dad's idea." They pulled apart, Chiyoko looking up with a sad resigned look in her blue eyes. "He refuses to let me graduate until I get a Ph.D. in education and take an appointment at his university."

FUNNY LOCATIONS

Warren glanced back, puzzled. "But he's at Stanford. He shouldn't have that much reach at this school."

"He's got an understanding with my credit card companies. But I've got enough spite left in me to study for art theory instead."

"Oh." Warren nodded at that. "But you're 23. You're old enough now to go live with your mom in Osaka, work for her maybe."

"I'd love to," Chiyoko sighed, letting go of Warren and turning away. "But Mom doesn't want me in the security business. She doesn't want her only daughter playing babysitter to some outfielder for the Kintetsu Buffaloes."

"Even though you've got enough martial arts training to star in direct-to-video action thrillers."

"Even though." She sat back down at her workstation. "But you're not here to talk about family. Are you here to beg for your job back?"

"I don't beg. And I have a job." Warren found a nearby chair and moved it closer before sitting down.

Chiyoko leaned forward. "So why come back?"

"Like I said, I have a job. Back in Florida. But I've been given something I've decided to do as a hobby."

She arched an eyebrow. "A hobby that would interest me?"

Warren arched an eyebrow right back at her. "For you, it would be more like an assignment. Yeah, a library job. It's perfect for you."

"Why just me?"

"Not just you." Warren leaned forward, lowering his voice. "But you've got the right qualifications."

She leaned closer. "For what? I need specifics. Now. I'm qualified to...?"

"To hunt. To capture."

Chiyoko leaned back, both eyebrows raised. "Oh. Work like that for a library would mean..."

"Yeah, that."

"Wow." She took a minute, breathing sharply through her nose.

33

Finally, with an almost wicked grin, she added, "And I will get paid for this, right?"

Richmond, VA
Yesterday

The laptop sat opened on the passenger seat, wires stretching from the power outlet and to a camera loosely secured to the dashboard. Chiyoko sat sulking in the back seat, having said her peace to Warren about the recent turn of events.

Warren's image flickered on the thin screen, his voice struggling against the static. Like all library projects, this one was operating tight against a small budget and working with aging equipment. "Chiyoko, I can understand your anger, and I am honestly surprised that Yoder was prepared for your team's incursion. But I think this does prove one thing."

Chiyoko leaned forward, tapping her wire mike dangling from her ear, close to her slightly scarred neck. "What would that be? That Bibliomaniacs have access to information on bomb-building?"

"That's old news, hell those books are one of the first things stolen." The laptop image cleared up enough to capture Warren's bemused look. "This proves these book thieves have a shared network, at least some form of organization. Argussen's case was never reported in the media."

Warren turned slightly at his end of the linkup, more than enough to face toward the driver. "Troy, I think we can use this information to better track them."

Troy Viator shrugged his broad shoulders, but kept his eye on the road. "First, we have to find that information."

New York, NY
Four Weeks Ago

"I think you've got the wrong office," the woman glared at

FUNNY LOCATIONS

Warren Stern as he stood there, shifting his head from one side to the next in bewilderment.

"I don't... but this should be..." Warren stopped, took a deep breath, and offered a specific reply. "I asked at the security guard's desk at the staff entrance. I asked for the rogue librarian's office..."

"And this is it," the woman interrupted. "Belle Sissner, formerly of the research office of the public library, now working as the web coordinator, and always have been a rogue librarian."

"I think he's looking for me." Warren turned to see the person he was looking for, a tall, broad-shouldered young man with shoulder-length dark hair and neatly trimmed beard. He grinned and offered a handshake. "Warren, what brings you to New York?"

"Troy." Warren shook his hand. "Man, what is going on here? I thought you were the rogue librarian..."

"I was, down in DC." Troy rolled his eyes and shrugged. "When I moved up here, well, Belle here claimed dibs on it. We arm-wrestled. She won."

Warren turned to face her, shocked. She smiled back smartly and noted, "There's more rogue librarians than you thought." Belle went back to work, humming the Spider-Man theme song.

Troy tapped his old friend on the shoulder, gesturing that they walk back into the administration hallway. "You should have asked for me at the reference desk. So, let me guess. You're on your quest again. I had heard you went looking for that Book With the Blue Cover down at that Florida library you're at..."

"No. Well, it wasn't there. Almost died, too. Hell of a mess." Warren shook his head. "I'm not here for that."

"But you're here for something else." Troy sighed, nodding his head as he considered something. "Same old obsessions..."

Warren leaned in close. "I am here for the best researcher on the East Coast."

Troy huffed. "Should have asked up at Arkham University."

"I'm not kidding. This is serious."

"Everything's serious with you." Troy turned and walked to a doorway, stepping through into a small lounge and gesturing for Warren to enter. Once the door was closed the taller man practically snarled. "I was there, remember? At the LC. When you quit. I still remember that shock on your face, that you were being forced out of the one place you've always wanted to work at."

"I'm not looking to get back in their good graces..."

"Every action you've taken has been. I kept up with you. That job in Texas, that brief foray with the new Library of Alexandria. Even that passion for that blue book quest, like finding that would let you back in."

"I left there, as a matter of honor, and you know it. And I know, I've known since I came back from Egypt, that I'm never going back." Warren scowled darkly. "Hell, I never asked you why you left the Library of Congress."

Troy stood tall, spreading out his shoulders. "Want me to tell you?"

"I'm not here for that. I'm here to offer you an opportunity that I can't fulfill, but that you can."

"Liar. You're offering me something to keep your hands clean." Troy turned for a moment, stepping away. "You're here looking for me. You want something researched."

"Yes."

"And what happens when I find what you're looking for?"

"Not what. Who."

"Who?" Troy faced him, puzzled.

Warren nodded, taking a moment before adding. "Book thieves."

Troy's eyes widened. "Dude, I'm no detective. I'm a librarian."

"You're a researcher. A damned good one." Warren took a step forward. "It takes the same skills, the ability to find, to know what to look for, which tools to use..."

"Okay, okay, wait." Troy turned about, making a circle on one foot a few times before stopping. "Who specifically am I supposed to hunt down?"

Warren took another step closer. "All of them."

FUNNY LOCATIONS

"That?" Troy scowled, and the snarl in his voice returned. "Oh, man, this one won't just get the hands dirty, but I'm seeing jail time at the end of this flakejob. You do realize law enforcement frowns on such vigilantism..."

"You can relax. We're not killing anyone. We're stopping Bibliomaniacs, and we're retrieving stolen books. It's not as unethical and you're making it out to be..."

"Well, that's not a straight-out confirmation of legality either." Troy lowered his head, thinking. "Something of this scope, someone's paying for it."

"Yeah. A special project."

"Who? We're talking a big special project."

"There's not that much money, if you're thinking about salary."

"No, actually, I'm not." Troy kept his head lowered. "I'm trying to think of who would back you on this."

"That's not the point." Warren took one more step closer. "The point is, there are book thieves out there, and I'm offering you a chance to stop them, once and for all. And I do know you. Not just the best researcher, but from when we worked together."

Troy kept silent, but glanced away from Warren, visibly upset.

"We talked, you and I. You ranted enough times about all the damaged books on every shelf. You got rather angry, more so than anyone else I've known, about every lost book you couldn't find."

Troy stepped back. "I'm not interested in some form of vengeance, Warren."

"Good. I don't want that from you." Warren nodded, offering a handshake of his own. "What I want is to give you a chance to finally do something about it..."

Gainesville, FL
Today

Argussen blinked, squinting against the bright light shining close to his face. He could hear the footsteps of the person who just now removed his blindfold, but he found he couldn't turn his head to see.

"Argussen?" A voice spoke close by. "You know why you're here."

"Let me go, man," the Bibliomaniac whimpered. "I have rights. You can't arrest me, I want my lawyer..."

"Ah, yes, that page we found in your pocket ripped out of a *Martindale-Hubble* directory. Well, we're not police."

"What? Well, then, who are you? WHO ARE YOU?"

The light turned away, and Warren Stern's face hovered close to Argussen's. "We're librarians."

"Oh GOD no," the bound man whispered, straining against the straps holding him to his chair.

"Tell me," Warren asked rather politely, "who Duncan Yoder is and where we can find him."

Argussen's face turned pale, then red. "I, uh, I don't know that name."

"Odd. He knows you." Warren leaned upright, stepping back from the chair. "I'm not above torture, not with the likes of you..."

The bound prisoner tried to laugh, which came out as a desperate wheeze. "There's nothing you can do to me."

"Yes there is. There's one thing that can break a Bibliomaniac." Warren nodded to his shadowy partner in the distance.

The light dimmed. Another bright image took its place. A row of televisions, each showing various episodes of *Seinfeld*.

Argussen screamed immediately.

Fredericksburg, VA
Two Hours Later

"And that's all he said?" Troy kept one hand over his right ear while shoving a cell phone close to his left. "What about where we can find Yoder?"

"He doesn't know Yoder's other whereabouts, just the one in Richmond." Warren sounded calm, almost contented. "But we do

FUNNY LOCATIONS

have the online networking sites they've been using. That should help you."

"Good." Troy walked toward the car as Chiyoko gestured she was finishing refueling it. "I'll check my email soon. And for God's sake, turn off those VCRs, I can hear the canned laughter in the background."

He slammed the cell phone shut. "We have info."

Chiyoko took the driver's side of the car. "Do we have Yoder?"

"No, but we can trace his connections, find another lead."

Troy slid into the passenger seat as she started the engine. "One other thing. Apparently, somehow they've been waiting for this a long time. The Bibliomaniacs must have realized librarians would fight back someday."

"And?" Chiyoko appeared unruffled.

Troy sighed. "Yoder was one of the more confrontational of their ilk, from what Argussen tells. He's ready, and he doesn't care. Quote, 'I will destroy all librarians before they take back the encyclopedias I've gained.'"

"Too bad." Chiyoko revved the engine, accelerating into traffic. "Here we come, Yoder. And we're taking back those *Britannicas...*"

TO BE CONTINUED?

SNIPE HUNT

Despite what people know, it does get cold in Florida. And no, none of the fun stuff like snow or iced-over lakes. No rolling white hills or frost-covered windows. It's all storm fronts blowing in from the north, bringing just the chilled razor-edged winds as a reminder that winter was still a part of things.

It was that kind of wind cutting through the citrus groves that covered the horizon as I pedaled my way to Guzman's place. There wasn't much to do in late January on a Friday around here except to hang out with your friends, and that was pretty much the plan the five of us had for the evening.

John had talked earlier at school about sneaking into one of the pool halls in town, but the rest of us nixed that, knowing full well they would be packed on cold nights like this one.

More than likely, we were going to stay in, play that new car chase game Guzman got for Christmas, and watch Billy Joe try to apologize to his ex-girlfriend for about two hours over the phone. Well, he wouldn't call it apologizing, and he might be right. It actually sounds more like groveling.

I crested the hill overlooking Guzman's place, the fourth house down the road overlooking an old scenic trout pond. It took a moment before I gripped hard on the handle brakes, seeing even from this distance all four of them waiting on their bikes in the driveway. John, Guzman, Billy Joe and Hack, just sitting there staring in my direction. Great. Someone made a change of plans. I hate changing plans, even when I'm guilty of doing it.

I let go of the handle brakes, letting gravity slowly drag me downhill into the driveway. I did my best not to sigh or grimace. "Yo."

Guzman shook his head at John. "I told you he won't be keen on doing it."

"Hey, hey, hey." I raised both hands defensively. "I'm perfectly reasonable to hearing what the new plan is before rejecting it."

John pushed his bike slowly, circling around to get to one side of me. "Would you really reject something as fun and enticing as a house party?"

"Naw, of course he wouldn't," Hack chimed in, grinning as always.

I arched an eyebrow at John. "There's no house party tonight. Anyway, we're in no position to throw one, our parents don't have the insurance for it."

John nodded with a sideways glance. "Oh, there's a house party tonight. One of those last-minute things my brother heard from his buds. Jase was invited, but you know his girlfriend Acee? Her parents are gone for the weekend, so he's... they got other plans. I say we crash in his stead."

I couldn't stop the scowl. "He's the one with the invitation, not us." I quickly realized something. "Wait, John. Jase's on the varsity team. It's gotta be one of their parties."

Guzman nodded. "Yeah. It is."

I faced John. "Ah, jeez. The varsity football team. The seniors, fer crissakes. They're not going to want us there."

"Why not?" Hack shrugged, still smiling. "We're going to be playing next year on the team."

"Right, but for now we're junior varsity, minor leaguers. We're

FRESHMEN, Hack! We'd be as welcome as deer ticks at an Agoraphobics convention!"

That, thankfully, kept Hack confused for the time being.

Actually, I wasn't too sure what I just said myself, but I knew words with more than three syllables would throw him off. I turned back at John. "If we go to a party we're not invited to, where there's a group of people who'll want to use us for target practice, we are going to get killed."

"C'mon!" John's voice went up to the octave level children use to annoy parents during long car rides. "There's gonna be beer there."

I closed my eyes. "We grab a can, we die."

"There'll be girls there."

"We talk to one, we die."

"Aw, c'mon, do you hate the seniors that much?"

"No." I opened my eyes to glare at him. "The seniors hate US that much."

John shook his head. "Stop exaggerating. We've dealt with the guys on the varsity squad before. They don't hate us. If anything, they're indifferent."

"That's because, when you were dealing with them, you're on school grounds and they're sober."

"Look, I say we go." John glanced around to the whole group. "It's a party. It's gonna be fun, a helluva lot more fun than just sitting around."

I did my own glancing. Guzman wore a slight scowl on his face telling me he had his doubts, while Hack went back to his slightly goofy expression because the concept of party crashing appealed to him. Billy Joe's face was the only one I couldn't decipher. He noticed I was looking at him, and he finally spoke up with that flat Mid-Atlantic accent his family brought down from Pennsylvania. "I know what you're saying, Liam. I know your concerns. And I think you're right. It's too much trouble if we go."

So of course, we found ourselves roughly two hours later entering Heckitt's house to the glares of a large gathering of older high schoolers.

John just didn't let up. He kept begging, and pleading, and needling, and harassing. He kept acting like we were going to the party every ten minutes, zipping up his jacket as he stood in Guzman's foyer, and kept acting surprised that we weren't moving. And he just kept at it. So we went just as the distant sunset shifted from orange to purple, biking down the side roads of Lake Wales until we crossed midtown.

Like I noted earlier, most of the older kids at the party immediately glared at us as we walked through the front door. One or two of them might have hoped we were bringing pizzas, but when that hope faded they glared at us, too. I don't think John noticed, as he blithely stepped from the foyer away from the crowded living room and toward the back of the house.

Hack followed like a minnow swimming in his wake, while Guzman and Billy Joe stood next to me with their hands shoved deep into their jacket pockets.

"So, any bets on when we get killed?" I noted quietly to my colleagues.

"Five minutes," Guzman muttered.

"No bet," Billy Joe added. He tapped my shoulder and pointed at the dining room just past the living room. "We've been spotted already."

I glanced over there to see a tall, broad-shouldered bald senior stand up and march slowly in our direction. Harmon, an offensive guard. His specialties included lifting Honda Civic coupes over his head, and holding a freshman getting a toilet head bath with one hand while juggling three golf balls with the other. "Okay," I muttered, angling my right foot away from the living room, "let's go this way and find a hiding spot."

I circled past the stairwell and hallway, sliding past a pair of teen girls indulging in conversation and through a partially opened sliding doorway into a room with books covering every wall corner. Guzman and Billy Joe stayed close as we hurried over to another doorway leading into a bathroom. A couple sat in the bathtub, kissing and groping and not paying us much mind. From there, another doorway led into the kitchen, teeming with teenagers constantly opening the fridge looking for cold cans and then the pantry looking for stale chips.

"Why don't we just get out of here?" snarled Billy Joe under his breath.

I glanced past him, noting that Harmon didn't seem to have followed us through the den. Still, it didn't feel safe. I shook my head, and muttered as best I could. "Like it or not, we can't leave with John or Hack. I'd feel guilty if anything happened to them."

"You would. I wouldn't. It's their fault we're here," Guzman answered.

"We could have still said no." I nodded in the direction of the archway leading to what looked to be the family room. "John's gotta be in there. Let's go."

I sidestepped past the open fridge door and the slouching beer-seeking senior in front it. I passed under the arch, quickly dodging someone shuffling around the nearby dining room table, doing what I could to make sure I didn't knock away that person's loaded-down paper plate.

A sudden loud chortling worked its way over the constant buzz you hear standing in the middle of house parties. I turned to see a tall group of seniors, each of whom I knew from sight.

They were players on the varsity squad; just the ones I knew we needed to avoid. Brian, who played outside linebacker and drove a truck bearing a 'NUNS R RDKILL' vanity plate. Willis, a skinny wide receiver who's usually okay to hang with, but is a lot like Hack in that he goes with the flow of the mob. Jorge, who played at tackle next to Harmon and rumored to have taught him that juggling trick, which I believed because his dad runs the corporate golf course outside of town, and because some of the smaller teens who work

FUNNY LOCATIONS

there on early morning shifts walk into school with wet hair. Schadendirk, the ringleader. Oh, God.

Schadendirk was worst of the lot, not because he was vicious but because his behavior didn't match the fact he was the bench-riding quarterback whose play-making skills were better suited to bowling. If he were a starter, then maybe, just maybe, it would justify the bullying. I haven't studied psychology yet and I'd probably need to win a football scholarship to a college that touts a highly esteemed degree in that field before I can make a professional assessment, but still I'm very sure this psychopath has got issues.

They were all gathered around the sofa, and I spotted a familiar junior varsity jacket being worn by a seated target. I couldn't see John's face from here, and I couldn't be sure how he was doing at the moment, but I could see the smiles on Jorge and Schadendirk's faces. It wasn't good.

Luckily, they were all focused on whomever they had trapped on the sofa, so I was able to get close enough to hear what the chortling was about. Schadendirk was doing most of the talking. "Just here for drinks and girls, then. Alright. Why not, guys?"

The seniors started chortling some more. I heard Hack's voice coming from the surrounded sofa. "Hey, cool. We're cool. It's a good party. Cool. Ya know?"

I spotted Schadendirk's smile disappear, which signaled the chortling to stop. "Even though you weren't invited?"

There was a slight awkward silence, and I stepped back fearing that someone would take the moment to look around and spot more freshmen. Schadendirk quickly smiled again.

"Like I said, why not? You guys are going to be on the varsity team next year. Might as well start acting like it 'round here."

He didn't stop smiling. "But you know, you gotta go through the motions. You gotta play by the rules. Being on the team, being a part of the team. Right, guys?"

There was a slight amount of chortling, but Brian added, "Being on the team. Yeah, right."

Schadendirk continued. "There's a lot of tradition on the team. To being on the team. I'm talking about getting initiated. The initiation. The rites and protocols." I was impressed he knew the word *protocol*. "When we were sophomores, we went through the rituals. Right, guys?"

More chortling meant confirming his statement.

"And I figure, 'Hey, you're here, you're going to be on the team, why not, right now, let you through one of the initiations?' And why not? You're gonna be on the team."

I heard an unfamiliar voice from the sofa, certainly a young timid creature speaking up for the first, and equally likely the last, time. "Can I go? Um, I not, you know, I'm not on the football team. I don't, um, I don't want to be... um." I spotted Jorge leaning in on his side of the sofa and reaching down, hopefully applying firm yet gentle pressure on the shoulder of whoever it was protesting his fate. Jorge usually applies pressure elsewhere on a person's body and in a rather painful way, but since this was a relatively public scene...

"I would think most guys would LOVE to do the initiations, boy." Schadendirk's smile turned a little too broadly, very much sinisterly. "Besides, once you go through the initiation tonight, you can proudly claim to be a man."

Brian laughed a little too loud for my tastes. I slowly backed up some more, not wanting to press my luck in avoiding detection. No one had yet to point me out, and none of Schadendirk's pals averted their attention away from the hapless freshmen they already had before them. I briefly wondered if Billy Joe or Guzman had fled for their lives yet, but I didn't have much time before Schadendirk announced his plans.

"Tonight, men, we will undergo the most important of rituals. Tonight, we snipe hunt."

I choked. Not because I was stunned by what Schadendirk said but because Harmon finally caught up to me and placed a big meaty hand under my chin.

FUNNY LOCATIONS

It was hard, riding in the back of Jorge's truck. He drove a little too fast when hitting the curves in the road heading out into the middle of nowhere, and the cold biting winds that had gotten sharper after the disappearing sunlight didn't make it any easier as my hair whipped into my eyes.

The best I could tell, even in the darkness and with half of my hair flapping over my eyes, Guzman was now glaring at me. I last spotted him glaring over to Schadendirk's truck about three road curves ago, where John had been placed. After getting captured by Harmon and a few other seniors he had recruited to round up all freshmen, Guzman wasn't too thrilled about how the night was turning out. He expressed his lack of excitement by throttling John before we were herded out the front door. Schadendirk promptly broke it up, his sadistic nature apparently requiring that we all be alive for tonight's torment, and decided on two trucks to drive us out to the middle of nowhere: Nowhere, the best place for a snipe hunt.

I count myself one of the lucky few that had an older brother who cared. While I was still in middle school figuring out how to blow up the first chem lab I had ever been allowed in, my brother Galen enlightened me with tales of being on the football team. Of special note were the fun, off-field antics that tended toward the bizarre, the kind of things teens would do when drunk and stressed over having to play Sarasota Riverview in the playoffs. This was how I'd heard of snipe hunting.

Galen himself was lucky as a youngster on the varsity squad, a prodigal running back not only popular with the girls in his class but also accepted with the seniors on his team. When it did come time to perform the snipe hunt, the seniors allowed him to stick with their crew while they herded his fellow sophomores into a darkened forest. After watching the ceremonial handing over of a burlap sack, he joined the seniors as they left the others who, under orders to stand there in the middle of the woods at night, would wait for the seniors to whack the surrounding bushes to scare out some timid, easy-to-catch bird called the snipe.

There actually IS a snipe bird. I looked it up. It's a waterfowl: You never find it in the middle of a forest. The encyclopedia I read also failed to note if the bird had an affinity for burlap bags, but there you go.

The whole hunt thing tends to be harmless. It's done in the middle of summer in more reasonable weather and in a location close to home so no one gets entirely lost. Everyone eventually gets drunk, first the seniors who pulled the prank and then the kids who straggle back in after realizing a few hours later that the whole thing's a joke. Galen told me a kid actually stayed out the whole evening in his junior year, and returned retaining possession of a rather tame Great Gray owl just as a search party was gathering to find him. No one knew where he got a Gray owl in the middle of Florida, and so the seniors figured he earned a few extra beer cans once the coaches weren't watching.

I shuddered, being reminded by the cold wind currents buffeting the truck that this wasn't the best possible weather for being out in the middle of nowhere at midnight, even in this state. Schadendirk wasn't really doing this to initiate us into the varsity squad. He was getting his kicks in tormenting someone, and he was just past the drinking point where he didn't give a rat's ass how deadly serious the whole thing could get.

The truck swerved again, the driver taking another turn of the road too quickly. I wasn't exactly sure where we were anymore, but I had a pretty good idea we were too far away from anything. We had been on the road so long it felt like we were in another county by now, well past walking distance to any safe haven I could think of.

At a point where it felt like Jorge was going to keep the truck in one direction, I stood in a crouching position and slid over to where Guzman was resting, atop the crossbed tool box locked into place underneath the driver's rear window. I heard a growling mumbling noise from Willis, left sitting near the tailgate to babysit us kids,

FUNNY LOCATIONS

Schadendirk thinking Guzman and I might be the troublemakers of the group.

The conversation where Schadendirk thought that happened just before Guzman vented his disagreement with John, and went like this: "Hey, do I know you? Liam, right? That new hotshot QB coach was talking about. Good to see you, short stuff."

Me: Not a word.

Schadendirk: "You listened in, I hope. Time to show you're part of the team, shorty. Hell, more than that if you're going to be the next big quarterback. Think you're up to it?"

Me: Doing the Silence Is Golden routine.

Schadendirk, after the smile faded from his face: "Speak up, Hannon, or Hammock or Hamster or whatever the hell your last name is. I wanna find out what you think of doing your initiation... right... now."

Me: "Got my name right the first time, but what I'm thinking is why your parents didn't change their last name to Smith or something, Schadendick." Which I know I shouldn't have said with a handful of 300-pound-plus bullies waiting to pound me into burger meat, but hell it had to be said.

So that's how I ended up on the back of Jorge's truck with Willis watching guard over Guzman, myself and the new kid. Hadn't even had a chance to learn his name yet. John, Hack and Billy Joe were in Schadendirk's truck behind us, which would recklessly speed up on the straight lanes as though they were passing but then pull back just before the road curved.

We sat and watched as his truck sped up again alongside ours, spotting a giggling Brian riding shotgun and our three compadres wobble back and forth in the back as Schadendirk swerved his vehicle like he was hitting imaginary road rodents.

I don't know why they weren't using Brian's truck: I guess they figured all the nuns would be off the highways tonight.

"You can never find the state patrol when you need 'em," I shouted to Guzman as we watched.

"I am not talking to you, bastard," Guzman growled. "And before you start arguing that I might actually be by the fact I'm saying words, let me just state for the record to all present that my earlier statement was a public announcement, that I'm continuing to make this a public announcement, and that my intentions are not to directly maintain any conversation with you. So shut up."

"Okay. I just wanted to say that we're screwed."

Guzman kept his mouth shut.

I lowered my voice enough to hopefully keep Willis clueless. "I know your dad keeps insisting you carry a Swiss Army knife at all times. Still got it?"

Guzman glanced warily at me, but no longer scowling. I interpreted that as a 'Yes.'

I kept the low tone. "I'm going to ask you to pull something. I know it's going to piss off these guys, and if we live through this they'll most likely pound us into the underground limestone. But I still say we leave a nice healthy 'Fuck You' to these bastards no matter what."

"Hey!" Willis tried to stand up to approach, but Jorge hit another curve in the road and it forced him to flop back down. "You two cherries break it up! I know you're plotting something!"

I took a moment to glare at Willis, then broke out a twisted evil grin. If you gotta die, die with your honor and humor intact.

I glanced over to the new kid. "Yo, dude! I want to ask you to do something for us!"

The new kid's eyes widened in shock, then he slid further down into the truck bed trying to find a hiding place. I took that as a 'No.' Well, damn.

Jorge made a hard turn with the truck, a sharp angle off the paved road onto what was obviously a dirt path of potholes, loose dirt, and other things that kill shock absorbers on vehicles.

The bright headlights of Schadendirk's truck as he pulled in behind us shone around the area, quick flashes of dark green and darker brown speeding by us. The short, large and lumpish shapes of the citrus trees we passed didn't show much past those headlights, but still I figured they were going to be dumping us in one of the big groves that take up half the county acreage.

I waited until Jorge slowed down his truck, taking a few seconds as he swerved to the right sharply and came to a complete stop. Schadendirk's truck slowly pulled over toward the other side of the dirt path, stopping in front of another dirt path going off into the dark. With the truck finally stopped, Willis stood up and started to move toward us. I whispered a few quick words to Guzman before the senior got too close, then with a swift jump reached over to the side and shimmied out of the truck bed. Willis shouted a warning, but you couldn't really hear much as Schadendirk had rolled down his vehicle's windows and was blasting some metal band music that sounded vaguely German except that the singer was growling in English. I kept picturing book-burning rallies using that stuff to set the mood. Call me old-fashioned, well I guess you should since I worship my dad's Blue Oyster Cult collection. Anyway, Schadendirk kept his engine running, kept the music blasting, and pretty much didn't notice as I got over to where Hack, John and Billy Joe were sitting.

The truck headlights were still providing enough surrounding glare in the grove for me to make out people's faces. John didn't appear too thrilled to be in the back of a madman's truck, and wasn't looking in Billy Joe's direction for some reason. Billy Joe seemed pensive, actually a little at peace with himself. Hack thankfully had a goofy smile on his face. He probably thought this initiation crap was real and he was going to be accepted as a brother by these guys. He was perfect for what I wanted to do next.

"Yo, Hack!" I shouted over the noise, getting his attention yet oddly not getting Schadendirk or Brian's. They were busy finishing off the Make-You-Deaf song. "Hack. Go get us some beers."

Hack glanced at me for a second, confused. When he finally processed the words *Get, Us,* and *Beers,* he broke out a lopsided grin and scurried out of the truck toward the driver's side. Schadendirk had kept a cooler in back passenger seat of the truck's cabin, obviously planning to finish off his maniacal plan with more drunkenness. I wasn't worried about Hack getting into any trouble asking for beer, even though the senior ringleader wasn't about to go sharing with us and most likely use an empty bottle to leave some painful reminders never to ask again. Even Schadendirk wouldn't kick at a puppy like Hack, actually he might. But not if a better, more satisfying target was at hand. I quickly circled around to the driver's side of his truck just to make sure the diversion would work.

Hack had just shouted out his request for brews just as I got close enough to see Schadendirk's reaction in his rear-view mirror. The senior quickly swung his door open, and interestingly the Open Door car pinging noise caught the down beat parts of the latest ubermetal song just right. The noise duet wasn't half bad. I made a mental note of it, planning to send the band's agent a suggestion they use Ford truck noises on their next album, hopefully when we get out of this alive.

Anyway, Schadendirk stood up from the driver's seat, trying to use his full height and bulk to intimidate Hack into cowering. Thankfully, Hack was both a reasonably good-sized defensive end, even for a junior varsity player, and also he was utterly clueless when confronting forces of darkness. Count it a blessing, I suppose.

Schadendirk deflated a little when he noticed Hack wasn't backing off, then squared his shoulders once he saw me standing off to the side. "Alright, then," he growled, stepping in my direction. "Your idea to ask for beer, Hamster?"

Got him real good and mad at me. I did my best not to show fear. "Why not?" I shouted over the noise. "If we're going hunting, I figure we're all going to need to quench some thirst before it gets too cold out here."

"You drink when I say you drink!" Schadendirk's voice was still raised at shouting levels even as the music cut off halfway through his roar. All that was left in the background was the constant pinging of the truck door warning. I spotted Brian getting out of the passenger side of the truck. A loud thumping noise from the truck bed just to my right caught my attention, and I saw Willis hovering over me. I could only hope Jorge and Harmon were closing in on the action over here. I returned my focus to Schadendirk, who now stood within half an arm's length from me. Close enough to smell the beer on him and realize it wasn't an Anheuser-Busch brand.

"Well, hey," I said, trying my best to be conciliatory and smarmy all at once, "I figured, we're all going to be like family with this initiation hunting trip, right? That's what you keep saying. Am I right?"

Schadendirk growled low, trying for a menacing whisper. "Try this, punk ass. You're not in until I say you're in. You're no hotshot on the team just yet. I don't care for your sorry ass and you haven't proven a thing to me that you're anything other than a snot-nose brat."

He pulled back slightly. "And yeah, for that dick joke earlier." He swung his left arm out, fist clenched, aiming for my face. "No goddamn jokes about my name."

His fist glanced off my cheek, grazing across the nose as I turned my face away from the blow. But his throw was weak, the punch didn't sting like I was expecting. I quickly assessed the situation, and decided on faking the apparent injury. I kept turning some more, angling downward until I dropped to the ground to my knees, bringing a hand up to my face.

"Gonna cry like a girl, bitch?" Schadendirk laughed loudly, enjoying the moment. He couldn't see me in the darkness feeling my nose and noting the lack of blood telling me that, like his gameplay, his aim was shoddy. "C'mon, Hamster, speak up."

I stayed down, keeping the hand up to my face. I could keep provoking him, but at this point I couldn't think of an entertaining and original insult to toss at him. I thought up a few variations on the "I'll see you in Hell" retort, but that just sounds so dull when you hear anyone say that. Anyway, Schadendirk doesn't much like the silent stare back response either. He proved that with a swift hard kick to my gut.

That one sent a lot of pain through my body, forcing me to kneel forward and grind my head into the dirt. After a few seconds of groaning, I growled through my teeth the observation that he should have tried out for placekicker.

"What was that, Hamster?" Schadendirk taunted, standing right over me, waiting for me to get up from my prone situation.

I heard footsteps, someone coming up on the other side from him, and spotted sneakers close to my head. The person knelt down, getting a good look in my eyes, and nodded with recognition and achievement. Guzman assuredly slapped my back twice, then gripped under my armpit to drag me to my feet. I glared for a second at Schadendirk, which changed to a look of false regret when I realized the glare would merely provoke him further, and answered. "I got the point."

The senior glanced between me and Guzman, who had let go and stepped off to one side. Schadendirk issued a quick chortle, that evil grimace of his flashing across his face. He feigned a backhanded slap at Guzman's face, then swung that hand onto my shoulder with a hard painful thwack. "Grab them," he ordered his compatriots. "Get the bags and let's go."

There was one good thing about being left in the middle of nowhere, Florida version, during a cold January night. No, wait, actually there wasn't. The night sky was clear enough to see every constellation I could remember from my astronomy classes, with a bright full moon giving us enough light to see the dark lumped shapes of orange trees surrounding us.

Schadendirk and his senior buddies had escorted us to this spot, cracking jokes about some obscure person back at high school, probably some other kid they bullied from time to time. We walked through the rows of citrus, feeling the wetness of sprinklers jetting

FUNNY LOCATIONS

out mists of water that locked the temperature surrounding the orange trees to just above actual freezing.

With the full moonlight, it had the look and feel of walking through a London fog. Did that once, family trip some years back. Galen kept cracking jokes the whole time about wearing a deerstalker cap and hunting down rogue mathematicians.

There was little sense of ceremony when Schadendirk picked the spot to leave us; an uneven, dug up dirt pile situated in the middle of a row of sharp angular tree shapes. From the moonlight, the surrounding trees didn't appear covered with leaves or anything, and the dirt pile sat in an open area that suggested a few dying orange trees had been recently uprooted.

Perfect. We were being abandoned in a dead zone.

Schadendirk didn't say anything as he handed Billy Joe and Hack each a netted citrus bag, not the traditional tight weave burlap sacks snipe hunters are supposed to wield. He waited for Harmon and Brian to encircle us, then finally made his big speech. "This is it. What you gotta do is simple. All you gotta do is stand here. That's it. Just stand here with the bags open and wait for the snipe birds to be flushed out."

I glanced at my compadres, having already learned this stuff. Guzman had his eyes closed, quietly shaking his head.

Billy Joe was glancing back at me with a skeptical eyebrow arched. The new guy shivered, probably because his windbreaker jacket wasn't doing so well keeping him warm right now. Hack was busy examining the bag netting, I swear it was like he was worried there might be holes in it. John was glancing back at Harmon.

The seniors circling kept fighting to keep their giggles from growing into guffaws. Schadendirk continued. "Now, the rest of us, we're gonna be doing the hard work, by going around and hitting the plants to wake up the snipe." I made note that none of the seniors were carrying any sticks. "That's the thing you gotta know about these snipe birds. They're idiots. At night they always fly low, always fly right out into the open areas. Makes it real easy to catch 'em."

"No wait," Jorge spoke up, trying to sound all serious at this moment. "There's something else these kids have to do to get the snipe. They may fly right at ya, but still you gotta entice them into your sacks."

"Oh, right, right exactly," Schadendirk picked up on that with a hearty chuckle. "To get them birds into the sacks, you gotta hold the bags wide open between your legs, and you gotta make the snipe call to convince them it's a safe place for them to enter. Like I said, these birds are stupid."

Jorge bent at the knees, demonstrating the position we were supposed to use, and he began making the worst set of smacking and clicking noises with his tongue. Brian completely broke into a loud guffaw, but the other seniors maintained their sense of decorum by sticking to their giggles.

"There you go," Schadendirk added as Jorge completed his demonstration. "Like I said, you kids get the easy part of the job tonight. You just gotta stand there and let the snipe come to you."

"You heard that?" Harmon growled from behind us. "You. Stand. Here."

"For how long?" Hack asked. Well, at least he was paying attention.

"Oh, uh, well until you get five snipes in each of those bags," Schadendirk shrugged. "Ten total, yeah that's a good number to work with."

The other seniors agreed to that. Willis started walking away back in the direction of the trucks. "Now, remember," Schadendirk said with all seriousness. "You have to wait here until you get all the snipe that we flush out for you. If you succeed, you're part of the team and you won't catch any shit from us. If you don't, well then, you're just not a team player and we'll make sure everyone knows what kind of wimp-wristed girls you are."

With that, we were left here, a cool mist surrounding us, and a bright moon overhead. I waited a few minutes, counting the time it took for us to get here to measure how long it took for the seniors to

FUNNY LOCATIONS

get back to where they parked. I didn't really think they were going to have anyone spy on us, being it was too cold, I couldn't imagine any of them volunteering to do it, and that they had beers waiting for them back at Schadendirk's truck.

Hack didn't wait too long before speaking out. "You know, I don't think they're going to find any snipe birds out here. You think?"

We took turns glancing at him with puzzled, disgruntled looks. I finally spoke up. "Okay, how many of you have figured out that this is a royal scam?"

Guzman: "Yup."

Billy Joe: "I was pretty sure they were leaving us here to die."

John: "Kinda figured it out, yeah."

The new guy: Total silence.

Hack: "Really? Then what's the deal with the bags?"

"The bags," I answered, walking over to seize the one in his hands, "don't mean diddly. These aren't even the right bags to use, and the whole thing's fake to begin with. This whole thing's supposed to be a prank!"

"Oh." Hack took a moment to process the data. "Then, how are we doing?"

"Not so good, if we're freezing our asses off," Guzman replied. "So what do we do now? Just stand here?"

"We shouldn't. We'll freeze to death."

"Not to nit-pick," Billy Joe replied. "I've been in northern climes worse than this, Liam. We're not exactly going to get frostbite down here."

"So? We're not exactly going to be rosy-cheeked and in good health in 20-something degrees of weather! Take a look up! Clear skies! Cold front blowing through! Take a look at the grove! They've got the sprinklers on to freeze up the trees before it gets TOO cold!" I handed the worthless sack back to Hack. "We should pick a direction and start walking. With luck we'll find a road, something to get a sense of where we are maybe. Like it or not it's a long hike back to civilization from here."

57

"Aren't they going to check on us, make sure we keep standing here?" asked the new guy.

"Like they care enough," I answered. "They're gonna want to finish off their beers and leave us here."

"What if..." John spoke up, a little hesitant. He spotted Guzman giving him an evil look, and he paused a moment.

Guzman shook his head and moved back a few steps. John eased up some, and continued. "What if we just go to them in a few minutes and just, well, I guess begging would be... well..."

"John," I sighed. "That's what they want. Either kill us or humiliate us. They don't care either way. We go begging, they win. For myself, I say no to that. I say we walk."

Guzman nodded in the direction the seniors left. "We ought to start moving anyway. I figure they'll come back soon. And not in a good mood either." He pointed in another direction.

"This way looks to be uphill. If we're in a good spot, we might see the horizon, spot some city lights or something."

He started walking, with Billy Joe following up. The new guy stuck with them. John kept pace with me as I followed, with Hack close behind us.

"Liam," John spoke lowly, "Uh, yeah. Look, I screwed up. Sorry, man."

"Don't apologize," I answered. "You're in the same fix we are, now. Let's just get the hell out of here, alright?"

"Yeah, well..."

"Just don't push your luck, until we get safe somewhere."

We caught up to Guzman, who had indeed reached a good spot atop a hill overlooking a lot of landscape. The moonlit horizon showed us a mostly spread out valley of trees, except in one direction that seemed well lit. A city, perhaps, or a neighborhood. At best those lights were to the farm running this grove.

"That looks promising," Guzman noted. "And it doesn't look that too far off. Well within walking distance."

FUNNY LOCATIONS

"And all that reckless driving must have been going in circles. Guess they didn't want to get too lost getting us here,"

Billy Joe mused. "All right. Maybe we WILL live long enough to see the Bucs lose to Philly in the championship game this Sunday."

I stepped past Guzman, heading in the directions of those lights. "Let's move."

We made it down that hill and reached what seemed to be a small worn out unpaved path before Hack amazingly asked an important question. "Why are we in such a rush here?"

"Well, like Guzman said," I answered, pausing briefly to look back in his direction, "we shouldn't really be waiting around for those jerks to get back to that spot. Anyway, we need to get out of the cold here."

"Wait, why would they be coming back to check on us? I thought you said something about them blowing us off?" Billy Joe asked. He glanced over to Guzman. "What is going on? You know something we don't?"

"Yeah, sorta," Guzman replied. "Liam made a quick suggestion before he bothered Schadendirk to share some brews. He made sure there was a distraction for me to sneak around and flatten some of their tires."

"What?!" was the instantaneous response from the other guys.

"They were pulling a prank on us," I answered, heading up another hill along the path, "so I pulled a prank on them."

"Well, hey, I helped," Hack added. I think the cold weather was improving his reaction time.

John hurried up from the back of the group to where I was, matching my pace as best he could. "You actually went and antagonized these guys? I thought you didn't want to get killed."

"It was, it is, a little too late for that," I replied. "I know I'm pushing things, but dammit I am not someone's stupid target. You know me. Remember the seventh grade, when that gang of idiots at lunch kept using my jacket for spitting practice? Ignoring them did squat, they kept doing it. This is the same thing. If Schadendirk's gonna pick on me I am going to fight back."

"Even if he gets worse."

"How bad do you think this is? Getting left out here in the middle of winter? This ain't a damn picnic. For all intents and purposes he, the whole bunch of them, left us here to die! Even if we don't, I ain't writing them fan letters tomorrow." I growled with right-eous indignation. "If flattening his tires is some escalation of hostili-ties, so be it."

I added a quick mutter under my breath, issuing a puff of steam into the chilled air. "I am not going to be bullied."

"Well, it hopefully might not be too bad," Guzman interrupted. "I mean, given the time and situation, I knew to only flatten one tire on each truck. If I did more than that I figured they would definitely hunt us down. Best of all, Jorge had a nail already in one of his tires."

That sounded good to me. "Really?"

"Oh, yeah. Must have gone in a certain way so that it didn't leak air out. Could be one of those tires with puncture-proof sealant. Anyway, I used my pocketknife to wiggle that nail out just far enough, heard the leak hiss out, so that should get it. Schadendirk's truck, I snuck behind Brian while he was watching you guys fight, unscrewed the cap and pushed the nozzle down to leak that way. So there's no actual physical evidence, I should think."

"Forget that," Billy Joe retorted. "Even drunk, they ought to be able to add two and two to get five." We just finished that Orwell novel in Lit class. "Still, you're right, Liam. We're going to get ragged on no matter what we do. Ought to be some way to tag these jerkoffs."

"Yeah, well." There wasn't much else for me to add to that.

Most of the other guys grumbled in reply. "What about you? Hey, new guy, what's your thought on all this?"

I knew he could speak, he had done so earlier, but he kept quiet this time. He must not like direct questioning or something. Billy Joe gave me a scowled glance. "Why do you keep calling him New Guy?"

FUNNY LOCATIONS

"Well, for starters, dude here won't give his name," I shrugged.

Finally he answered, rather sheepishly. "Name's John. Heckitt."

"Okay." I stopped right there. "Heckitt? That was your house you got dragged out of?"

We all turned to face him, and he nodded pretty quickly, embarrassed by the whole thing by the look of it. Billy Joe added to the querying. "Does your brother Jason know you're out here?"

"Probably. I dunno." The kid shrugged, like his being ignored or misplaced by his older brother was normal for him. "I didn't see him anywhere downstairs. Like he'd care, half those guys are his pals anyway."

"I've got a pretty good idea he'll start caring the minute your folks get home without you there," Guzman replied, giving him a hearty slap on the shoulder. "Alright, mission objective, guys, saving the rookie here."

We resumed the march toward the horizon lights. I glanced to the John already established within my posse. Yeah, my posse, my rules, my game show, etc. "We already got a John here. We're gonna need to think up a nickname for you, Heckitt."

"What? Why?" His protests came a little too lightly, a little too slowly. The other guys started with their suggestions right away.

Hack: "Iceman!"

John, the Original: "Hardcase."

Billy Joe: "Steve?"

The suggestions flew out pretty quick by my compadres.

"The Dicer!" "Lemon!" "The Pride of Polk County!" "Sebring Racer!" "Mouse!"

"Whoa, wait a minute," Guzman interrupted with that last one, stopping to glare at Billy Joe who had offered it. "Mouse? That's a little demeaning, ain't it?"

"So? I mean, look at him!" Billy Joe pointed with both hands, like a priest offering blessings or a car salesman promoting a Camry. "He's shy, diminutive, reasonably inoffensive, probably likes cheese..."

61

"Well, I mean, there you go, making the assumptions. And that 'shy, inoffensive' stuff is definitely demeaning..."

"Excuse me," came a whispering, inoffensive voice. The new guy was glancing between Guzman, Billy Joe and myself. "Um, why can't I, well, choose my own nickname?"

We glanced between ourselves and bobbled our heads waiting for someone to present the answer. Finally, I noted, "No one chooses their own nicknames. I mean, if you did, everyone would call themselves 'Ace' or 'Stud' or whatever. Naw, you get the nickname foisted on you and you live with it or you don't."

"Well, it's... But it's not exactly fair is it?" He stared right at me. "Did you like what Schadendirk called you?"

"Well, no I didn't." I scrunched my face for a second. "But that's different. He's an asshole."

John, not the Original, kept staring back at me. I took a moment and realized he wasn't seeing the difference. And damn if he wasn't right, all things considered. I sighed, shaking my head. "Fine. Fine, you offer up a nickname. But you gotta let us okay the choice, right? Put it to a vote."

The kid nodded. Then he stood there for about a minute, obviously thinking it over. "Oh. Okay. Um, any suggestions?"

We groaned, and started back walking towards the lights, which were now a few hills away from the look of things. John, not the Original, matched my pace and asked again, "Why it is so important that I have to get a nickname, anyway. Why not your friend John?"

"Oh, I've got a nickname," John the Original spoke. "Got it back in the second grade, with guys I used to hang with. Hated it. You don't want to know it. The friends I have now are good enough not to repeat it. I hope. Consider yourself lucky if you can get yourself a good nickname, so keep thinking of something."

"Why not just call him by his last name?" Guzman offered.

John, not the Original, gave it some thought. "I dunno. Too professional sounding."

"Yeah, that kinda sorts you right," Billy Joe nodded to Guzman.

FUNNY LOCATIONS

The kid glanced back. "He called you Hack, right? How'd you get that nickname?"

"Well, hey, that's what I do. On the field anyway. Don't mind it, sounds good enough," he smirked. "Real name's in the yearbook, unfortunately."

"What is your real name?"

"Don't ask!"

"It's kinda sad," I noted to him. "Parents reportedly lost a bet or something."

"And don't go looking for it either!" Hack snarled.

"And, then, they call you . . .?"

"I am William Joseph," Billy Joe intoned with all seriousness. "But we're south of the Mason-Dixon now. Interesting how I got to be called Billy Joe. Got my nickname from a school bus driver."

John the Original spoke up. "Refresh my memory, was that the one who kept telling us to sit down and shut up?"

Billy Joe gave him an evil glare, but we all ended up laughing for a good while.

The lights we were seeking were now close enough to better the moonlight, but the interesting bit was the music working its way over the landscape. Someone playing a radio or sound system, couldn't quite place the style of music just yet. As we headed closer to the sounds and the lights, Guzman kept up with the nickname suggestions. "Well, I gotta ask you, what's your thing at school?"

"My thing?"

"Yeah, you know, you in a sport, you in a club, you good at math or languages or what?"

John, not the Original, looked down at his shuffling feet. "I'm in the band," he grumbled.

"Marching band?" asked Billy Joe. "Dude, I hope they didn't stick you on tuba, those brass tubes are bigger than you..."

"Oh, no, everyone kinda knew not to let me on an instrument that big," the kid shrugged. "Actually, I'm on saxophone."

"You any good?" Billy Joe followed up.

"No, I suck."

Hack tried to pull a snarky comment. "I thought you're supposed to blow."

"That's the problem."

Well, damn, quick comeback. Kid's got a sense of humor. We all cracked up, getting a good laugh out of that. "Good one," I noted. "Alright, you're in the band. Can you think of anything music-related that'd be good for a nickname?"

I could see him scowling in the brighter lights we were facing flooding over the crest of the hill we were upon. "Well, a sax is a brass woodwind instrument. There's music, rhythm, tempo, beat, what else, words to describe music..."

"What about the instrument?" asked John the Original. "You do more than blow through it, right?"

"Well, yeah, there's pads and levers, gotta keep it clean from all the spit that goes . . . Wait. There's the reed I gotta replace all the time. How's that? Reed."

We stopped in our tracks, just a few feet from the hill crest. I glanced around to my buds, checking to see how they were thinking on it. Reed. Sounded about right, he was thin enough. "Okay, I'm cool with it."

Billy Joe: "Cool with it."

John, now back to being John: "Cool with it."

Hack: "Cool with it."

Guzman: "More than cool, damn I'm freezing. Is it getting colder?"

Reed shivered: In fact we all seemed to be shaking a little much more than usual. "Keep moving," I growled, and we turned back toward the horizon and rushed up the hill. We got to the top and looked into the source of light and music within this grove.

It was stunning in a way, something unexpected. This long, wide sheet of back-lit white covering that stretched along the side of the hill facing us. A wind would seemingly cut across the surface, rippling like a lake not yet frozen over. The ends appeared to be

FUNNY LOCATIONS

tented at the corners, held down by large construction trucks working as anchors. Other cars and trucks encircled the white tenting, some of their headlights providing the misty glow reaching up over the hills. The music that had echoed across the citrus grove rolled around more clearly in this dale, a salsa beat from what I could tell.

"Reed," I asked, "can you tell what kind of music that is?"

"Best I can tell," he answered, "is that it's loud."

That earned a stern glance, but not a long one as we joined Guzman and John hurrying down the hill. Hack swept past us, running in fact with the momentum pulling him faster downhill.

"Party!" he grinned, and sped past Guzman for the lead.

As we got closer, I could see past the bright lights to spot the shapes of people milling about, gathered together under the white tent. I heard the rumbling of an engine, undercutting the music some, and spotted a generator next to one of the construction trucks. A group of men, bundled down with heavy jackets, were sitting near there, and they pointed and waved toward us as we came within shouting distance. "¿De dónde lo hizo chicos vienen? ¡Tiene frío fuera aquí esta noche!"

Guzman waved back to them, and gestured that we go over and speak to them. "They're wondering why we're out here in the grove."

"Why we're out here?" Billy Joe queried. "What about them? Why the party out here?"

Guzman waited until we got close enough to get a conversation going without shouting too much over all the party noises. The men sitting around at this corner were noticeably migrants, certainly ones hired to work these groves. First or second generation by the look of things. We probably knew their kids at school. Guzman nodded to one of the guys, probably someone he'd seen at his dad's auto shop from time to time. "Fuimos abandonados aquí por idiotaes. ¿Por qué tiene usted un partido en la arboleda?"

"Los tubos de la agua en este lugar están defectuosos. Tenemos que utilizar las calentadoras," came the reply. Guzman continued discussing things in Spanish, and I found myself distracted by a change in the music being played. It had switched from a fanciful Mexican dance tune, I think, to a more recognizable techno dance track. I also found myself distracted from the cheering noises that accompanied the music shift: it sounded like girls.

I felt a tap on the shoulder, and turned back to face Guzman. "Get this. The pipes broke on this hill, so they can't use the water mist technique to preserve the trees. They broke out those old heaters. Apparently, someone who came up from Panama had this huge set of leftover parachutes from that Noriega showdown. Wonder how he got them through customs, but anyway. They thought they could trap the heat underneath the parachutes, so they set up this tent."

"Could you check to see if anyone might have a cell phone handy?" I asked.

"I could check."

John stepped over. "Could you check to see if we can get invited in while we wait?"

Hack stood right behind John and nodded vigorously.

Guzman slapped his forehead with some justifiable frustration. "Oy. Alright. I'll check."

"And see if we can get beers?"

"Beers? Las Cervezas?" came a response from one of the migrant workers sitting nearby. He broke out a huge grin, issued a quick laugh, then added "Debo pensar chicos que jóvenes no deben comenzar un hábito malo. Supongo que podríamos permitir que usted tenga una cerveza. Sólo un." He raised one finger to make his point. "Una cerveza."

John and Hack both whooped and hurried into the party. Billy Joe shrugged and followed. Reed walked tentatively into the area, but toward one of the heaters sticking up from the ground between some of the citrus trees nearby. I stayed with Guzman while he asked about for a phone or for some help.

After a few minutes, Guzman waved one hand at the guys and stepped back. "Okay. They suggested I check with their kids here, one of the teens ought to have a cell phone. As far as getting a ride home, we could ask the guy who brought the sound system here, he's got a good-sized van."

"We're not too far, are we?" We walked toward the gathering underneath the parachutes. Reed was keeping himself warm next to the heater, but I couldn't see the others within the crowd.

"From town? No." Guzman pointed toward the opposite corner, where a smaller group of people stood. "The coolers look to be over there. They didn't tell me how long the party was planned for, so I don't think we should wait for the DJ to pack up. There's enough transport here, someone's gotta be willing to offer a ride back."

"Yeah, actually I don't know how long we should stay here..." I replied. As we got closer to the cooler, I saw someone turn to face us, a young girl I thought looked very familiar. I think she smiled at us, and turned back around to the cooler. When we got closer, she had turned again, this time with two beers in her hands.

She offered one to me and the other to Guzman. She kept smiling, especially in my direction. "Hi, guys. Liam, I heard some stories about you tonight."

I recognized the voice: Jade. She of the green eyes, who sat two seats behind me in History and Civ class. She had done up her hair in a ponytail rather than keeping it loose around her shoulders like she does in school. I kept noticing her smile was staying right where it was, and I suddenly wondered why she and the friends sitting next to her were giggling half the time during the bits in class about the Reformation. "Oh. Yeah. Some of the football seniors dropped us off in the middle of nowhere."

"Really? Whatever for?"

Guzman took a swig from his bottle. "Snipe hunting."

"Oh." She kept her eyes on me. "Catch anything?"

"What? No, of course not. You're not supposed to catch anything." I felt a little off about saying that. Like what, try to say something impressive rather than truthful? Why did I even just think that I HAD to say something impressive?

"Oh, too bad." She winked, kept smiling, and turned away to head off to a group of girls who were giggling furiously just off to the side. "Well, good luck catching something next time, Liam."

Guzman kept silent, working off his bottle for about a minute while I kicked myself mentally. Finally, he sighed, slapped my shoulder once and muttered "That could have gone better, man," before heading off into the crowd.

I sighed and started on the beer in my hand. I think I heard Billy Joe's voice over the music at some point shouting "He did what?!" but I wasn't too sure. After the second sigh, I quickly realized three things.

First, I wondered if we were going to recover our bikes at Heckitt's house. Well, whomever drives us back ought to swing by there first to drop off Reed and all. But I doubt if the bikes are going to be in any pristine shape.

Second, I found myself worrying about what happened to Schadendirk and his buddies. Are they still stuck out there? Did they switch the flat tires with spares? Were they stupid and drunk enough to try and drive home on flats? Part of me still didn't want to give a rat's ass about what happened to them. The other part of me was certain they had fixed their flat tires and had gone back to Heckitt's party to commit unspeakable acts to those bikes from Thought One.

Third, I realized just because Jade walked off didn't mean I had to stand here like an idiot. I placed the half-finished bottle atop a pile of crates and hurried off in her direction. I ought to at least make sure I understood exactly what she meant about catching something.

WELCOME TO FLORIDA

Welcome to Florida, where it's perfectly normal to wake up to a bale of marijuana in your driveway.

I spotted it coming out the front door seeking out my morning paper, couldn't miss it if I wanted to. The bale sat there, wrapped in blue packing saran wrap, three feet from the gutter, placed there quietly and politely like a Christmas gift. Had to be four feet by five by six in measuring, a pretty large shipment of Mary Jane.

I glanced about examining the neighborhood, wondering and worried about witnesses, if I had a chance to slide this oversized package to a hiding place. I counted a handful of people up and down the street. Some of them neighbors I know and chat with from time to time. Each of them glancing my way, at me and at the bale. Realizing I'm now stuck with the problem, I sighed and strolled as casually as possible as anyone could towards something that could cost you twenty years in a well-fenced federal prison.

I spotted my morning paper, sitting atop the bale where the delivery guy must have placed it. As I made a calm, measured effort to grab the banded newspaper, I made a cursory examination of the packing. Nothing torn, no corners dinged, no sign of damage to the wrap. I could see through the blue tint that inside the wrapping were individual bags, each about a foot long and tightly packed with herbs, shredded remains of marijuana leaves. It was all well-packaged and hand-delivered with care. I glanced at the paper in my hand and idly wondering if the St. Pete Times was doing another promotional give-away. Part of me was hoping this was just a massive shipment of oregano and that this package was meant for a neighbor planning the biggest spaghetti cookout in state history.

"Must be one hell of a party you're planning there, Bob." I turned, recognizing the voice of my next-door neighbor Brad Jassik. He stood next to his Lexus, already dressed for work, heading out for that long commute across the bay to his law office.

"You know me, Brad," I answered, shrugging and shaking my head, "I usually order a handful of dime bags for my parties. Besides, there's so much here I doubt even all of Jamaica could finish this off in a month."

"Good point." Brad took a sip of his coffee. "Seriously though, you buy dime bags of pot?"

I didn't look at him, glaring instead down the street at the handful of neighbors still standing and watching me suffer in public. "I'm being sarcastic in the face of potential arrests, you bastard."

"You might want to hold up a sign over your head spelling that out next time," Brad chuckled. "Well, it's in your yard, you gotta take care of it. Thinking of sharing?"

"You asking?"

He shrugged. "Noooooot really. But I gotta admit it's pretty brazen to have that sitting out in the open like that."

"Very brazen, but not my idea," I agreed. I took a step toward him and aimed my thumb behind me toward the bale. "Just to make sure, this um isn't yours by any chance?"

"Ha!" Brad snickered and turned towards his Lexus. "Good luck with it," he states with an over-the-shoulder wave at me.

Watching him drive off, I returned my attention to the bale of pot still sitting in my driveway. There was one unshakeable thought:

FUNNY LOCATIONS

How did this get here? Each solution seemed crazy when I mulled it over. If there was a chase involving cops, with the dealers dumping their load, the cops would have made an effort to circle back and get the evidence. There were no sirens or screeching tires last night either. If the cops weren't involved, if it were rival gangs chasing and fighting over this shipment, someone still would have made an effort to recover the bale. We're not a drive-through neighborhood, there's no reason for traffic to be passing by, and the packing doesn't look dinged or crumpled, so this couldn't have been an accidental spill. If it was a delivery, you'd think the dealers would make more of a discreet effort, not leave it out in the open like this. Best thing I could think of, this was a problem involving a wrong address. Well, a wrong address and someone abusing their own supply. You can't expect potheads to keep their information straight, anyway.

The next thought bouncing through my skull was "HEY, what do I do with a quarter-ton of pot in my driveway?" This being Florida, I had some options.

The safe play was to call the cops, but that as well posed risk. This size of shipment, the cops are gonna want to add a person, someone convenient, to it to show off a shiny arrest to go along with it on the nightly news. I sighed to myself. This is when those youthful indiscretions working on an alt-music magazine during your college studies twelve years ago come back to bite you on the ass.

Keeping it was a bad idea. For all the joking I did with Brad a minute ago, I really don't care one way or another about pot use. I grew out of it after college, didn't need it now. I wasn't about to begrudge someone's else use as long as they didn't deal to kids or anything. Hanging out with potheads back in college, I knew all the stories and arguments for pot. For the most part, I agreed about the medicinal value. Recreational... Nah, I didn't need it.

The other thing to consider was that this was a huge-ass pile of pot. Someone, especially someone with a truckload of invested money and a truckload of armor-piercing bullets, is bound to miss it. Even if you make the safe play of calling the cops in to take it away, what happens if the persons interested in this much happy weed come back looking for it and are displeased with how it got taken away?

I had to make a moral judgment on this. So I went looking for the wife.

Markie was still working a cup of coffee, building up the energy needed for the day at her job with Raymond James. It was that job that brought her to the state three years ago, all wavy blond hair and bright blue eyes, totally unprepared for what Florida living really meant. It took that first weekend we went out together on an arranged dinner date when I escorted her back to her place, where an alligator had gotten into her second-story apartment. Markie it seemed grew up in a friendly small town in Indiana and had never considered how leaving the screen patio door unlocked wouldn't deter unwelcome guests.

"HOW THE HELL DID IT EVEN CLIMB UP HERE?" She screamed, glaring at the sedate and serene gator sitting in her bedroom, from the safe distance of the apartment kitchen. "LOOK AT THOSE STUBBY LITTLE LEGS!"

"Relax, Markie, okay? Try not to aggravate the poor thing by yelling at it..." I offered a soothing tone, rubbing her shaking hands while we waited for Animal Control. "As for, well, getting here... Gators get to act a little, um antsy when it's mating season."

"NOT ON MY BED THEY DON'T!"

Markie settled down a bit by our third date, and thankfully by our wedding day she'd gotten used to alligators to where she didn't attack the one that camped out near the wedding cake. Having a handful of other crazy things happen to her since relocating to Tampa has gotten her... well I wouldn't say "jaded," perhaps that she's more "attuned" to how Florida can warp one's mind. Yeah. Attuned is the right word.

"Ahh, Markie, love of my life," I cooed into her ear, wrapping her from behind with my arms, "I've got some good news and some bad news."

FUNNY LOCATIONS

"Oh God no," Markie groaned. "Not another dead campaign pollster on the doorstep. Please no."

"No, not that bad. There's a bale of pot in our driveway."

Markie slowly lowered her mug to the counter, shrugged my hug off as she turned to face me. "I'm gonna assume that's the good news."

"Well, that's still up in the air." I locked my gaze to hers. "It's not yours, is it?"

"Oh please." Markie paused. "How big is it?"

"About the size of a Honda Civic."

"Definitely not mine." She closed her eyes and pointed instinctively to the wall phone. "Call the police. Non-emergency number."

I reached for the phone. As a form of perfect timing, there was a knock at the door.

Markie arched an eyebrow. "Damn. That's the fastest I've ever seen the cops around here move."

"That could be the bad news," I answered. "It could be the owners showing up for it."

Markie got up from the counter stool and scurried toward the bedroom. "Gun. Got it."

The knocking continued. "I'm gonna answer the door."

"Okay. Just remember to duck out of the way, husband."

"You just remember not to come out shooting if it IS the cops," I answered back. I worried she didn't hear me.

The pounding at the door continued, persistent but not aggressive, as I approached. Through the smoked glass, I could recognize the shape of a tall, thin, terrifying figure. With dread, I opened the door.

As I feared, it was the neighborhood snoop, Mrs. Carterwall. Eighty years old and somehow taller than I was, neither the pace of time nor weight of age nor enforcement of restraining orders have stopped her from poking that hawking nose where it didn't belong. "I hope you've called the cops," she stated with the authoritative air of that third grade teacher we've all had and hated. "You better have called the cops about that filth in your driveway."

"Ah, ma'am," I answered with false politeness. "Trust me, my hand was on the phone as you knocked."

"Well you better call." She put a hand to her chest, over where a heart would normally reside. "I'D call if I could, but those fools don't take my calls anymore. Not after those letters I've sent to the papers about their incompetence."

I just nodded, keeping my lips pursed. You try not to say too much to her, or provoke her into prolonging any diatribes.

"And of course, even if you called about the fight, I'm sure they won't come. Just wait until someone bleeds all over the place, or even die, I wonder if the cops will come then!"

"Wait, what?" I raced past her. "What fight?"

I hurried back out to the driveway and stared in dismay. Two figures stood, armed, angered, ready for war.

"Back, you harlot!" screeched Mrs. Kittner, a retiree from Pennsylvania that the whole neighborhood knew was suffering a horrific case of glaucoma. She waved her walking stick as high as she could, aiming for something she couldn't really see well.

"It's mine, you undersized bat from the Ninth Plane of Hell!" Mrs. Anderjacque stood a foot taller than her opponent, and she raised her husband's 3-Iron as high as she could, which wasn't too high. "My cancer treatment! Mine!"

They started circling and waving their weapons at each other. Kittner couldn't hit anything being as blind as she was. Anderjacque couldn't keep the golf club higher than her hips.

"See?" Carterwall spoke as she strolled alongside me with an air of smug justification. "See what drugs do to a fine community like this?"

I turned to face her and pointed my hand toward her house, that dark place that had dead rose vines and purple-tinted exteriors. "Go. I will take care of this. Just get out of here before the cops show and the cops arrest you."

"Arrest ME?" Carterwall lifted her chin, defiant. "Whatever for?"

FUNNY LOCATIONS

"Trespassing. Again. NOW GO!"

Carterwall shuffled about three feet from me, wrapping herself tight in her blood-red morning coat, but refused to shuffle any further. I shook my head in frustration, and turned toward the battling retirees. "Ladies? Ladies can I have your attention?"

"NO!" Both Kittner and Anderjacque kept swinging with remarkably poor aim at each other.

I seized the golf club from Anderjacque and glared at her well enough to force her back. Kittner crowed and tried swinging her cane again, but I grabbed it and forced it down to the concrete. "Stand. Still," I growled at her.

Kittner growled back but kept the cane by her side.

"Now, ladies," I sighed, glancing between them. "I take it both of you were expecting a..." I paused, looking at the bale sitting between us. "Delivery of some sorts today?"

"It was actually due last week," Kittner growled. "I have glaucoma, you know. I need this for my eyesight!"

"Oh, screw your glaucoma," Anderjacque snapped at both of us. She yanked at the shawl over her head, exposing bald spots with side patches of short white hair. "I'm getting cancer treatments, and I've been waiting for this shipment so I can induce a hankering of munchies back into my life after all this damn chemo!"

"Mine!" screeched Kittner, and the cane went back up.

I grabbed the cane from her. "Stop it! You get this back when you promise to stop hitting people with it."

"Like she's already hit anyone," Anderjacque muttered.

"Oh please, please," Kittner started a begging routine, not a very convincing one at that. "Please sir I need this, this is mine don't let anyone..."

"Shut up you cow," Anderjacque started interrupting.

"ENOUGH!" I shouted. Both women went quiet. "Fine. Wait here."

I stormed back to my garage. Digging through my clump of junk, I spotted two necessary items: A machete and a wheelbarrow.

75

PAUL WARTENBERG

Grabbing both, I rolled the wheelbarrow back down the driveway. Carterwall spotted the machete and screamed "MURDER!" and thankfully ran as fast as her fluffy bear slippers could handle.

Anderjacque was able to see the machete as well but said nothing, waiting to see what I did with it. Kittner squinted her eyes through her glasses, before asking "What the hell you breaking your lawnmower out for?"

I didn't answer, pushing the wheelbarrow past her and sliding it up next to the bale of pot. Raising the machete, I hacked into the blue saran wrap, taking a few blows to begin cutting into the plastic. Yanking apart the open slit, the individual bags of pot spilled from the bale. I tossed the spillage into the wheelbarrow, and pulled a few extras out from the remaining pack, until I was certain I had evenly divided the bale. I lifted the up the wheelbarrow's handles and shoved it toward Mrs. Kittner's house.

I reached it and dumped the pile onto her driveway, near the garage door. I rolled back and dumped the remaining bags from the bale into the wheelbarrow and rolled it to Mrs. Anderjacque's down the other end of the street. Dumping it there, I turned back around and returned to my driveway.

The two ladies glared at me, well Kittner tried her best to glare but she was focusing more on that palm tree on the other side of the driveway, then at each other. Finally they huffed and muttered together, "Fine."

"Fine." I raised my hands at both of them. "And next time, please, for the love of God, while I'm not accusing anyone or anything, just make sure your dealers get your damn addresses right." I rolled the wheelbarrow back to the garage, put the machete where I found it, and stormed back into the house.

Markie had returned to the kitchen counter, gun next to the coffee mug. "So, I saw you settled the matter. Think that's it for a crazy morning?"

"Not unless Carterwall adds anything more to it," I groaned.

"Humph." My wife took a sip of her coffee. "Should have shot her when I had the chance."

I slid into the kitchen stool next to her, placing my elbows on the counter and holding my head up with a much needed facepalm. "Ahh, honey. Let me tell you, it's official."

"What is?"

"I'm getting too sane for this place."

"Oh, hon, that's not true." Markie took another sip. "If you were sane you would have kept that pot and sold it off Craigslist."

That got a chuckle out of me. "You shouldn't be encouraging me to do something illegal, hon."

"True. You should let your accountant do that instead." She placed her mug down, turned and gave me a gentle hug. "You were sweet to do what you did, though. I love you, man of mine."

I gave her a kiss. "Keeps me going, hon."

She sighed and leaned back. "I just wonder, who the hell's package was that?"

"Don't know, right now don't care," I whispered. "The only thing I wonder, what the quality of the pot was."

The cops told us later. "Oh, yeah, Canadian quality," the arresting officer said as his fellow officers were dragging Carterwall off for possession. Kittner had called to complain about someone grabbing at her stash when she wasn't looking. "Not any homegrown closet-grown crap, lemme tell ya. We already grabbed the dealer who dropped it off, we found him in that Wal-Mart parking lot sleeping off his late-night buzz." The cop shook his head. "Delivering while on his own stash. The only good thing about dumb criminals is that they are DUMB when it comes time to find them."

The wife and I stood back and watched the chaos as three cops shoved a handcuffed Carterwall towards one of the police cars. "Why are you arresting me?" she wailed. "Those women were the ones who have those drugs on them!"

"Lady," the arresting officer placed a hand on her shoulder, shoving her into the back seat of the patrol car. "Considering we got you dead-rights possessing five bags of pot and we got ten different witnesses using phone cams to document you stealing those bags, you got no right to complain! And consider this! One of these women is a decorated military veterans with a medical history of glaucoma. The other woman's that suffering chemotherapy just happens to be the daughter of an appellate judge. There's no WAY I'm gonna go through the media shitstorm arresting either of them will get!"

The officer slammed the car door shut before Carterwall could get another whine in. He noticed us standing nearby. "Seriously. It stuns me how people think they didn't do anything wrong even after you slap the handcuffs on them."

"Florida thing?" Markie suggested.

"Nah. Cop thing." The officer nodded. "Ma'am. Sir. Have a nice day." He turned and noticed the neighbors circling the cop cars. "Move along, folks! Nothing to see here! Just another drug bust in the suburbs! Move along!"

"Gods, I am soooo late for work," Markie whispered to me as we strolled back to our home.

"Call in sick," I whispered back with a smile, "I'll call it in to my office as well. We can take the day, just curl up at the pool and not think, not do anything but just laugh at the whole crazy morning."

"Ahhh, husband," my wife smiled and leaned in, wrapping a soft hand behind my head as she lifted herself up on her toes to kiss me. "I knew there was a reason for marrying you. Well, other than your gator wrestling skills."

We both giggled as she slid her arm back under mine, clasping my hand. "Think this will make the front pages tomorrow morning?" Markie asked.

"Probably not," I answered. "This is Florida. Unless the drug dealer they caught was an elected official or something."

Which it was. I never voted for him though. It still only made the Metro section of the paper. At least the FARK site tagged the story. They live to write about the crazy stuff that happens here.

WHERE THE SNOW IS GRAY

It was for Jenny the one argument too many with her mother. This time the shouting and throwing of objects was taking place in the grandparents' home. This had been the teen girl's sanctuary, ruined now as Jenny's mom ignored the rules.

"ENOUGH!" Jenny flashed the rage within her eyes. "This isn't about Dad, this isn't about my brother YOU never told me about! This is about YOU! ABOUT YOU BEING A BITCH!"

Jenny didn't wait for the screeching reply. She ran, taking a second to reach the porch doorway, wrenching it from its hinges, letting it dangle like the leftover of a tornado as she leaped off the wooden deck onto the hard cold ground.

Jenny ran, ignoring the screaming insults that followed. What else would her mother say to her after all, what else was worth noticing? Jenny ran, her sneakers pounding into the frozen mud of her grandparents' dirt driveway. Jenny ran, the speed and power of her athletic frame carrying her as fast and as far as she could.

The woods were stark green firs draped with white clumps of morning snowfall that shone in the early afternoon sun. They shaded the teenager as she ran, and it never before occurred to Jenny just how long a distance the driveway was.

The gate at the end of the path stopped her. The lock was still on, as Grandpa had not gone on his business into town yet that day. Jenny pulled and pushed, letting the chain and lock rattle, feeling the burn of her muscles and enjoying the vent of her anger against something that could take the blows. On the third pull she felt something give, a pole on the fence perhaps, and she paused. *I've got to stop breaking things*, she realized.

Jenny considered jumping the fence. It'd be easy. She knew her athletic skills.

But, Jenny thought with a clarity she missed since receiving the news about Jake, *where would I go?*

A noise behind her caught her attention. She turned to see headlights, a truck: her grandfather's. It would be so like him to come looking after her. But Jenny's mother would be in the truck, she'd insist on coming along.

Jenny ran. There was a clearing between the property fence and the small forest that made up the Foster homestead. An easy track over the sloping hills of the mountain valley across the snowfall.

The fence continued even as the county road curved away from the property and towards the nearby town. For a brief distance, barely half a football field, the woods surrounded both sides of the fence clearing. Then it gave way to an awe-inspiring view of an open field. High white fences bordering her grandparents' functional barb wire surrounded an open pasture beneath snow-capped majestic peaks glowing in the clear sky sunlight.

Jenny saw it but didn't let it register. Her tears were not enough to block the view but her anger was enough to keep her from thinking about anything other than running away from her torment.

Her hot breath turned into mist as she ran alongside the fence, no sign of fatigue. Hot tears cracked against her cheeks in the cold as she ran. The snow turned gray from the shadows of her grandparents' forest, casting over into the white hills of the pasture behind the

FUNNY LOCATIONS

pretty fences she used as markers to gauge her distance. She was not getting far enough away, and it bothered her to where she couldn't think a single coherent thing.

Jenny didn't even realize she was running alongside a horse farm, ignoring how her presence disturbed a herd sniffing the land for graze. One of the younger horses took her passing as a challenge. The young horse raced up to match Jenny's pace, his head bobbing as his legs churned against the snow-covered ground.

Jenny at first refused to notice. It had been years since any pretty pony caught her eye. Given how it was one of the few things her mother bribed her with as distractions, Jenny was not in the mood to be reminded of that. When she let it sink in, that here was a handsome creature sharing in the moment of speed and energy, her anger churned faster than her legs.

Before she knew it, Jenny ran faster. Faster than the yearling.

The young horse did his best to keep up, matching her and keeping his bobbing head and bright mane within the corner of her eye, but it infuriated Jenny into racing like mad.

The colt slowed up by the fourth hill. By the fifth hill, Jenny saw why. The open field closed off as the white fence angled away, leading to a large muddy work area, flattened down by trucks and equipment and frozen days. A barn stood in the distance, half a field away from a three-story Victorian home with large porches, open windows, and friendly Christmas lights draped everywhere.

Other people, Jenny thought. It snapped her out of her focused anger. She slowed to a walk, strolling up to the barricade between the forest and the farm. The barb wire fence here had disappeared for some reason, the poles remained standing but no cords dangled against the wooden fence, making it safe to approach.

Jenny climbed up, perching herself on the top rail, swinging both legs around to place herself in the neighbor's yard and not her grandparents'. Nearby, the horses strolled over the hill, watching what this odd human would do next.

Jenny waited for a few minutes, breathing hard. The long run was finally catching up to her as the intense drive to flee her mother's faults faded. If grandpa's truck showed up she could just start running again. The stark beauty of the winter horizon reached her, and the teen spent the moments marveling at the distant mountain range beyond and the bright blue sky above.

Movement at the barn: From this distance Jenny could only tell it was someone tall, with unkempt raven hair wearing a black jacket. He seemed familiar. At least he waved a hand-tip salute in her direction.

It wasn't smart of her, but Jenny wasn't in the mood for smart. She hopped off the fence, splatting her shoes into mud. Walking in his direction, the teen got close enough to recognize his face from a few nights before.

He walked towards her, that lopsided grin easy on the eyes. "I know you. Heather's friend, the out-of-towner. Jen?"

"Jenny." She stopped and he stopped about five feet apart. "You weren't lying."

"About what?"

"Being neighbors." Jenny glanced about, nodding towards the horses now gathering at the fence to watch. "I thought there was an older gent who owned this, didn't have kids last time I was here."

"Oh, yeah. That was my uncle Ulmer." The boy frowned for a moment and shrugged. "He passed away, more than a year ago. Been sick the year before. Aunt Gemma, she wasn't up for... Ah, anyway my dad had an interest in horses and figured, what the hell, we'd run a farm." He grinned with awkward humility. "We haven't gone bankrupt yet, so we're doing well."

Jenny tried smiling for the first time that day. "Hate to say this, but I forgot your name."

He nodded. "It's Scott." He pointed a finger at her. "Jenny. I'll try to remember."

"Thanks, Scott."

"So. Out for a walk?"

"Actually, I've been running."

Scott half-turned towards the farmhouse. "Interested in a quick tour of the place while you're visiting?"

"Sure."

They walked side by side. Two steps in he asked, "How do you know Heather, you mind me asking."

"I grew up here." Jenny wiggled her head. "Well, for a few years my grandparents took care of me, while... mom was off on business. Third and Fourth grades. We stayed in touch." She bumped her elbow against his. "How do you know Heather, if I may ask."

"Ah. Painful to say."

Jenny arched an eyebrow. "You dated her?"

"Not that well." Scott scowled.

"You don't know her that well?"

"No, I didn't date her that well."

"She never mentioned you."

"Yeah well, that's not a surprise." Scott stopped, still scowling, finally shook his head and sighed. "First attempt was at a bonfire party, we got attacked by wood scorpions. Second attempt..." He sighed even deeper. "Her friend Lisbeth... kinda... threw up on half the movie theater."

Jenny squinted in shared sympathy. "Ouch. The gods showed no mercy."

"Yeah well, we didn't want to risk a third try." Scott winced at the memory. "It wasn't even a scary movie."

"What was the movie?"

"*Mannequin.*"

A door opened in the short distance. A jacketed figure stepped off the porch and into the afternoon sun. "Scott? You didn't mention friends coming over."

"Mom." Scott put up a half-hearted wave in her direction and muttered in Jenny's direction "Whatever you do, don't ask for any horse rides. Mom charges. A lot." Scott grinned back over to his mother. "Hey, this is one of our neighbors, walking by."

"Running by," Jenny muttered back.

"Oh yes, of course!" Scott's mom had a wider face than his. Still tall for any woman at five-ten. Jenny wondered at what age Scott outgrew her. "Your grandmother, she talks about you. And thinking on it, did your grandfather say you were in cheerleading? Oh, wait, marching band!"

"Oh, that was a long time ago," Jenny tried to laugh a bit, putting a hand over her mouth. She resisted telling how she didn't last very long as a flag-waver after that sword debacle during band camp. "Actually, I play on the volleyball team. State title this year. Not here, but back home at..." she let her voice trail off. She wasn't sure at the moment she had a home left to go back to.

"Here for the holiday season, then." Scott's mom grinned. "Out for a walk."

Jenny decided not to correct anybody on that point.

Scott took the moment to speak. "I was thinking she came by to see the horses, but I was going to show her around the farm instead, if that's all right."

Scott's mom gave him a look, took an interested glance at Jenny, gave her son that look again. "You do know you've got chores around the barn, and getting the equipment looked at?"

"Mom, I know!" Scott's voice took the tone of a teenager with a parent negotiating over the details. "Tour's part of the chores." He circled his mother, reaching for a set of large tools sitting on a bench next to the porch. "You know, just to talk and explain about some of the stuff I do around here. She can do the talking, since I'll be busy, okay?"

Scott's mom glanced between Jenny and her son. "Chores gotta be done, that's what I'm telling you."

"I know. No distractions." Scott leaned in, his arm around her shoulder. "Mom, this isn't like having the guys over while I'm working."

"Oh, that's saying something," Scott's mom grumbled in a disapproving tone. She muttered something in her son's ear, which Jenny easily heard as "no funny business."

FUNNY LOCATIONS

"What's wrong with having the guys over while you work?" Jenny quizzed Scott as he escorted her towards the barn while his mom stood and watched the pair.

"Hm, you might not know the guys." Scott scratched his hair with his free hand. "Still you lived here once. You go to school with Jake Henks, maybe Wilford Twoharp?"

"Names don't ring a bell, no. What are they like?"

Scott grimaced. "Kinda like having a gas lamp next to Mrs. O'Leary's cow, which was something they tried re-enacting the last visit they ever had here."

Jenny winced. "Banned for life?"

"Easy to do when it's Wil. He's in jail now." Scott swung the barn door wide to make room for the two of them to enter. "Best not to talk about what he did for that."

To Jenny's suburban nose, the whole barn smelled of horse. "You're not going to have to shovel much during this tour, are you?"

"Oh, been done this morning. Already mucked out, the step I gotta do now is spread the straw over the stalls, that's the bedding." Scott walked past a set of large tubs and pointed upward as he headed for a ladder. "Kind of take a bale from up there and knock it out into the stalls below. Watch."

Jenny watched from the ground floor while Scott did his work above. With a large hook he had grabbed earlier, he dragged a bale with ease over one stall, and with a push of his boot let gravity do the rest. The bale exploded into the stall, covering the existing straw with a fresh layer. "Hey, do you want to grab a pitchfork there and spread that out a little? See how it goes?"

"You want me to do your chores for you?" Jenny snarked.

"Not at all," Scott grinned back. "Just this one stall. You can tell all the city kids back home you worked in a barn."

"They'll be so jealous." Still, Jenny grabbed the pitchfork and went into the stall, flattening the lumped remains of the bale until the new straw mingled and overlapped the old. "There. Do I get a hay certificate now?"

"Paperwork will take weeks," Scott answered from above. He had spent the time dragging over another bale for the adjoining stall. "I'll wait until you're out of the way down there."

"Stall has walls, I'm not gonna get hurt."

"Didn't want to scare you." Scott waited until Jenny walked away from the stalls before dropping the next bale in. "So, what do you think of the exciting life of a farm boy?"

"There's got to be more thrills than this," Jenny answered, taking a few steps towards the ladder. "You get to ride the horses for free, or does your mom charge you for that?"

Scott chuckled somewhere overhead. "I work for a living around here, pays for the room and board. Besides, I prefer riding my motorcycle."

Jenny padded her way up a few rungs of the ladder. "Must be the life, riding on that through the hillside, up and down the mountains."

"Yeah well, I stick to the paved roads. Any riding around in the woods is asking for trouble." Another thud in the stalls as a bale plumped to the ground. "Especially during tourist season."

Jenny's head poked over the balcony. "Also hunting season, I'd expect."

Scott was busy dragging another bale, but stopped and turned to her with that grin of his. "Same season around here." He resumed dragging the bale. "Nope, better off coping with crazy drivers."

Jenny finished her climb, rested atop a bale as Scott did his delivery. She stared at him, stone faced and bothered by his comment. She knew he was joking, and that he wouldn't know her family. It wasn't his fault what happened to Jake. She sat and waited for him to walk back for the next bale.

Scott stood, looking at her, breaking out an almost-shy grin, swiveling over to sit on the bale next to Jenny. "Bored already?" he asked.

"Not bored, just," Jenny sighed, "thinking."

"About?"

She glanced at him. "Family."

FUNNY LOCATIONS

The two teens didn't say anything for the next minute, alternating shared looks. Finally, Scott turned and glanced in every direction along the floor and hay bales stacked around them.

"What are you doing?" Jenny asked.

"Looking for wood scorpions."

"Feeling a little awkward?" she laughed.

Scott stopped glancing around and looked at her. He seemed entirely earnest. "Just a little. I mean, supposed to be doing chores and here we are just chatting about, well I dunno what but..."

Jenny pressed her kiss a little hard into his face, catching the top part of his open mouth. He quickly relaxed his jaw, angling just enough to make the kiss softer, her nose brushing a cheek bone.

The kiss turned into a series of quick lip-mashes, which turned into frantic groping at jackets. Jenny tried to unzip Scott's while he wrapped an arm around her back, sliding her into his lap. She was struggling with the zipper snagged halfway down his chest when Scott leaned back and whispered "Why are you crying?"

Jenny opened her eyes. Scott was close enough she could see the reflection of her own flushed face in his gaze. She reached up a hand, wiping away at the right side of her cheeks, then the left, still feeling more tears welling up in the corners.

"I..." Scott paused, then lowered his forehead to brush against hers. "Are you okay?"

Jenny nodded, tried to laugh but stopped when she felt it become more of a sob. Sniffling made the moment more embarrassing. She pushed herself slowly out of Scott's lap and onto the bale she'd been sitting on, only to tip over and flop with a girly shriek onto a layer of spilled hay.

She lay there, fighting off tears, as Scott rolled atop the bales. His face hovered over hers. "I get the impression you're having a day."

Jenny groaned, rubbing her face with both hands before dropping them down to her belly. "Oh God. Oh, I'm just... This is crazy. I'm crazy. I'm just... There's all this stuff in my life and now and I, and there's... I just needed to feel something good for... I'm sorry, I didn't mean to..."

"If you're apologizing for the kiss, don't." Scott grinned. It made Jenny want to reach up and pull him down for another go. "But if there's something else going on..."

"It's just me." Jenny tried to laugh again, then frowned. "I'm going to end up like my mother. I can see it. I'll do something stupid, and get pregnant, and go crazy dealing with a guy crazier than I am, and God knows whatever else like get drunk and get stuck in rehab and, God, get into shouting matches with my kid and do stupid stuff like ruin everybody's lives."

Scott offered a serious look. "Are you pregnant right now?"

Jenny raised both eyebrows at him, then chuckled "No. Pretty sure of it."

"Are you drunk?"

Jenny shuffled her body, placing her elbows to arch her shoulders up. "No."

"Do you drink?"

"Not yet."

"Well then, you've an incentive not to start," Scott grinned. "Trust me. I've watched my older brother come home from frat parties stinking of beer and then collapsing in the bathroom after puking his guts out, and this one time he did it where his body blocked the door so we couldn't get in to check if he was still alive. Terrifying night. Well, he sobered up by morning, but after that I was thinking to myself 'Where's the appeal?' I mean..." He laughed, and Jenny had to smile at that.

"Well, you've got a point, I'm not exactly there yet in life." Jenny sighed. "You've got a good-sized family then. You get along?"

"With my sister, mostly. Terry's back east in Virginia, where we moved from. Married a guy from college, already has a little girl, She's a handful." Scott shrugged. "If we're talking about parents, they're okay. Dad's strict, I'm still in the doghouse with him over, ahh stuff, but Mom's there to talk things down."

FUNNY LOCATIONS

"I don't have that." Jenny felt how wrong that sounded. "There's my grandparents, they're okay, but when it comes to my mom it's... it's not a good thing."

Scott looked at her for a minute. "I'm not my brother. You're not your mom. Maybe it's not that simple, but..."

A voice from below the balcony. "Scott?"

"We're up here, Mom!" Scott lifted himself up on the bale and looked over his shoulder. "We're just talking!" He leaned back down at Jenny and whispered, "Not at all a fib, I mean we ARE just talking right now."

"Just now, yeah." Jenny giggled. She blinked fast, realizing there were still tears in her eyes.

The voice of Scott's Mom echoed across the barn rafters. "Is it just the talking, or rolling around in the hay?"

Scott grimaced. Jenny sat herself up and shouted as best she could. "I'm the only one rolling in the hay, Mrs. Scott's Mom. Besides, I couldn't get his jacket unzipped."

It was worth it just to see the blood drain from Scott's stunned face. There was a long awkward silence that really only lasted five seconds. "Figures," Scott's Mom answered back. "Can you get down here, Jenny?"

Jenny stood up and brushed off her backside, knocking straw off her pants. "Wait, did I tell your mom my name?"

Jenny moved slow down the steps, while Scott waited above. Scott's Mom stood with a stern expression, *but at least her arms weren't crossed in disappointment* Jenny noted. Once Jenny got close, Scott's Mom leaned in to half-whisper to her. "I got a call from your grandmother."

Jenny's stomach twisted.

"They were worried you'd gotten lost, was asking around, your grandfather remembered you talking with my boy a few nights back." Scott's Mom leaned in a little further, like she was wanting to drape an arm over the teen's shoulder. "They said there was a ruckus but that it's okay now, and that you ought to head back in maybe another hour after the anger's cooled down. Are you gonna be all right?"

Jenny thought about it. "If it's okay for me to stay for an hour, then yeah."

Scott's Mom smiled and leaned over with a quick hug. "Just stay out of my boy's way. He's got chores, I'm not kidding." The woman looked up. "SCOTT. CHORES. NOW!"

Jenny knew the rest of the day went too quick, especially the brief ride on Scott's motorcycle back to the grandparents. The gate was unlocked this time, telling Jenny the welcome would be civil. Except as Scott reached the front of the house, Jenny counted an extra car that worried her.

"Who's this?" Scott braked, placing one leg out to balance his ride.

Jenny spotted a smallish human lump wearing a thick hood and jacket, swaying on the porch swing. "I have no idea."

"You ready for this?" Scott asked as Jenny slid off the backside of the cycle.

"Probably not, but I'll survive," Jenny answered, placing a hand on his shoulder. "Lean over." She kissed him, soft and long. "Give me a call. So we can talk."

"Deal." He saluted, revved up the bike, and swerved back down the driveway.

Jenny watched him pass over the small hill out of view, then turned her attention to the human lump on the porch swing. A few steps up, she could see it was a boy, middle schooler, rapt attention to an electronic device in his hands. "Who are you?"

The boy didn't answer, focused on the device.

Jenny walked closer. "Who are you here with?"

A flinch from the boy. "My dad."

Jenny blinked. "Is your dad Linus?"

"I guess." The boy's device was a Game Boy, one of those fancy

FUNNY LOCATIONS

handhelds from the year before. It seemed like the boy had an early Christmas this 1990. "He's inside, been shouting at a woman. Used to be mommy and daddy to some other kid."

Jenny scowled. This wasn't right, not after what she'd been told earlier. *All that fighting had been over a mistake?* "Are you Jake?"

"What?" The boy actually looked up from the game, then realized his error and refocused attention. "No. My name's Ken."

"Wow. Dad has another son," Jenny muttered, more to herself than to Ken. This new sibling looked to be too young to have been with Dad's other ex-girlfriend, which meant a third woman was involved. "Huh. Dad's seed is a powerful and prolific force."

"What?" Ken noticeably scowled, the implications lost on him.

"I'm being sarcastic." Jenny smiled anyway, and walked over to try and take a seat next to her half-brother. Ken flinched, glared at her for the brief second he could afford, and pushed his butt against hers to shove her away. "Excuse me. Busy."

Jenny laughed. She considered leaning over to kiss his forehead and embarrass him further, but she didn't want to get off on the wrong foot with this one. She sat and watched Ken fidget under the unwanted staring, then with a smile, rose up and crossed the porch toward the kitchen door.

She found Grandpa working on the door frame. A new screen door rested against the wall, tools and bits strewn across the porch. "Oh, hey Bunny," the old man nodded, busy with a screwdriver.

"Heya Pops." Jenny stepped gently over the parts, making her way over to the other side where she could kneel down to him. "Damage to the door, huh?"

"Nothing that can't be fixed," Grandpa answered, groaning a bit.

Jenny examined where her forceful slam had shredded half of the frame. "Ah, that was not good. Didn't know I was that strong. I'm sorry, I didn't mean to wreck the home."

"Oh, no bother." He finished remounting a door hinge before turning to face his granddaughter with a smile. "Door's been rusty for years, needed the excuse to replace it anyway."

"Hey, still saying it's my bad," Jenny smiled back, and offered a hug. "Let me help at least."

With the kitchen door open, it was easier to hear Jenny's mother and father grumbling in the living room. Jenny couldn't tell exactly what was being said. "Who called Linus over?"

"Your mother, which I told her not to do," Grandpa scowled. "Still, Kelly needed to find someone else to yell at after you went running, as though you'd have gone over to his place." He waved a gloved hand toward the living room. "That idiot father of yours is living on the other side of the mountain range no less, like you'd have gone that far in ten minutes."

"I dunno, I think I might be a good runner," Jenny noted. "I'd just fly away."

"You didn't. Good thing the wife called the neighbors. I told Elise you'd been talking with the Monaco boy, figured you'd go that way when I saw you run off at the gate." Grandpa felt around the deck for something. "You see the drill? Gotta work on the top hinge next."

Jenny glanced up. "That wood's no good, Pops. Need to cut out the frame and remount a new piece of cut wood up there."

"You think?" He struggled to stand up, Jenny standing with him to get her body under one shoulder. "Hate to think it's going to take another hour or three to get this, daylight's already going."

The shouting inside erupted, fast and loud. Jenny flinched, refusing to head inside, knowing it would make things worse. After a minute of chaos, both voices went silent. But the wood flooring of the whole house shook as heavy steps thundered down a hallway.

"He's leaving now," Grandpa muttered, shaking his head.

Jenny patted his shoulder and hurried around him, back to the front of the house. She got there just as Linus was grabbing up Ken by the arm and dragging him off the swing. "Dad?"

The man turned and looked at her. It'd been years since Jenny had seen him, and since then he'd become smaller in her eyes. It didn't help he was down the stairs and halfway to his car. He pushed Ken to the other side of him, and raised an angry finger in his daugh-

FUNNY LOCATIONS

ter's direction. "You've pretty much ruined everyone's day today, haven't you, princess? God, what the hell did Kelly think when she raised you up to be just like her, an obsessive me-me-me witch..."

Jenny's mom stormed through the still-open front door to shout. "Wouldn't you know, first words out of your mouth to your own daughter is to insult her! You don't care, you never did..."

"ENOUGH!" Jenny silenced them both. She could feel Grandpa's hands on her shoulders, steadying her, and saw that Grandma had come out to wrap an arm around Jenny's mom, with a few whispered words to keep her calm. Jenny frowned at her mother. "Mom, we can yell at each other later, but I gotta ask Dad something first. And Dad..."

Her father raised the finger at her again.

"Just stop that, Dad," Jenny interrupted him. "Just answer me this one question, and go away. Just tell me. Where's Jake?"

Jenny's father flinched. "Why the hell would you care?"

"Because he's my brother," Jenny answered. "Because I need to say hello."

Jake was at another town down the highway, and Jenny's grandparents drove her there the next day. The cemetery was stark, with fresh morning snow blanketing the trees and markers. It was a nice place for mourning, a sloping hill overlooking a creek feeding out of a mountain's frozen waterfall a mile into the distance.

The grandparents waited at the truck while Jenny counted down the spots to where Jake would be. There was some open space there, for Linus' side of the family perhaps, with Jake the early arrival.

Jenny brushed off the snow, reading the dates of Jake's lifespan, a Biblical passage etched into the stone from John 14. She knelt, leaning in, wondering if he would be there to listen.

"Hey. We never met. It's been kind of crazy in my life, what with Mom and Dad barely talking and half of it stupid, well anyway I just only found out about you yesterday Jake, so I'm sorry if this is a bad time to be meeting and all. Did Dad ever talk about me to you? Did you know? I mean, about us. That I'm your sister. It'd have been nice to have known you, maybe if you weren't as crazy as Dad is. It'd have been nice to talk. To see if there was someone normal. You know, in our family."

She spent an hour at the grave, where the clouds cast a dark shadow. Snow fell, covering herself and Jake in the gray, but her happy talk with her brother kept her warm.

THE HIDE AND SEEK SUITCASE

I keep bringing it out for my travels. This year it's my trip to Vegas and the Grand Canyon. Driving there and back. I need room for the clothes I'll wear, and pocket change for the laundromats along the way.

I keep forgetting what it is I hide in this damn thing.

Every year it's the same thing. I realize I left something from the trip before in that suitcase, and I forget exactly why it was that I had that in my luggage. This summer I dread what it would be, as the trip to Washington did not go according to plan. Well, not to my plans. Blame it on my travel partner.

The suitcase is long, gray cloth with zipper pouches everywhere, rollers at one end and a collapsible handle to the other. Tossing it on the bed is hard as the weight of it bothers me. I feel a lump in the middle, hidden behind the zipped-up flap. It's bigger than I remember it being.

I pause with the zipper. Drawing a breath, I realize I need to do this. If I don't, it just means I need to buy a new suitcase and leave this one in the closet dust. Besides. I have to know for certain. The zipper parts as I yank the tag, swift and smooth. Nothing caught between the teeth. Folding the flap over and away from me, I gaze in awe at the lost item now found.

It stares back at me, baleful, contemplative, golden. How I got that Egyptian burial mask out of the Museum of African Art, for the life of me I still can't recall.

I hate it when my brother gets me drunk and in the mood to pull heists. I swear, every time, whether it's New York or Paris or Milan or that nice little place in the Andes. What starts off as a tour of micro-breweries turns into wacky escapades that flummoxes the FBI and Interpol. And I'm always too drunk to remember how clever I could get, each time.

Damn it all. I ought to stop sharing these trips with him. Then again, we are going to Vegas this year. A view of the Grand Canyon up the road during sunset is one of those bucket lists, after all. I mean, how often can you plan a decent scenic road trip between the coasts?

I lift the mask with both hands and consider what wall anchors I'll need to put this up in the gaming room. Might as well. It's not like it's something I can take back to the Smithsonian Lost and Found desk.

I promise myself as I put the mask aside and clear out room for my socks. This year will be different. I don't care what my brother says about this place he knows that makes the best lagers. I won't get suckered into another round of criminal escapades. I mean it.

THAT LAST MINUTE THING

Wake up. I forgot something.

Fall out of the bed. I kick at the blanket to get free and stand up.

The clock says Two A.M. and the world is sleeping except for me now. I press my feet to the wood floor, feeling for my flip-flops. Once they're on I can stumble out into the house and not bang my toes against the furniture. Only coherent thought I got at the moment, aside from wondering what the hell it is I've forgot.

The house is dark. Light switch to bedroom is near. With the light on I can see the living room and kitchen. Easy to dodge furniture now. Still bang a flip-flop into the bookshelf. Only toppled those old Bloom County collections to the floor. Need to shelve better. Head for the kitchen.

Drinking coffee right now a bad idea. Stick to water. Get the throat wet, get the mouth feeling soft and fresh. The chilled water strikes my body a way that turns my awareness up a notch. Still thinking about what it is driving me out of my sleep.

It's got to be something I need to do. Wait. That means a schedule. A plan to follow, and a date as deadline. Right, check the calendar.

Tomorrow, right there on the paper, but it's just one word. Birthday.

Oh crap. Someone's birthday. I forgot, like an idiot I forgot. I need to get a present.

No way I can go to sleep now. Must shop, get this taken care of.

Pants and clean shirt. Got to get dressed, going out in public with just underwear does not go over well. Learned that in college. The shorts dangling off the dining room chair will do, need to find the shirt. Shirt found lumped near the bed, passed the sniff test. Shoes on. Never trust the cleanliness of a retail store.

Keys. Wallet. Smartphone in case I need to call for help if I lose my keys and wallet at store. Get another drink of water in the system. There, ready to go.

The store is a fifteen-minute drive, at this time of night not much traffic out here in the outer circles of suburbia. Just me and one drunken speedster, has to be drunk as he's weaving more than I am, and my excuse is just drowsiness.

Parking lot at the Knotts Mart with just two rows of cars lined up diagonally closest to the two front doors. The K letter flickers, either that or I'm blinking too much. Need the retail sections, the housewares and toys and games and electronics stuff. The groceries section not important. Someone else is getting cake. I hope.

Head through the Enter sliding doors on retail side of store. Greeter seems half asleep like me, but he offers me a cart with wobbly wheels. "Welcome to Knotts-Mart, for all your shopping needs. Looking for anything in particular?"

I mumble. It's almost English. "Urm luffing four a something other thingee. Uh, birffday."

The greeter keeps smiling but he has to take a moment to figure out what I said. "Oh, a birthday! Is this for a friend, a family member? A child?"

FUNNY LOCATIONS

Glance into the store and shake my head. I mutter something along the lines of "Aye huff null idea."

Refuse the cart. Just need to buy one thing. Just need a present. Thingee. Walk in, check which direction is best to go. Head left, toy section there. Maybe figure out whose birthday it is as I get there.

Way is blocked. Flag standing in the middle of the aisle, how did it get there? Someone claimed towelette aisle for the glory of Uruguay. Need to salute so as not to offend before walking around it. Try not to trip on it.

I get to the toys section. Too many action movie figures and cheap knock-offs of ninja turtles. Where are the fun games anymore of my youth? Wait. Think. Shopping for a child or an adult? Memory not working. Stroll down the aisle, see what catches the eye. It's all blurred. Part of it panic, part of it also panic. Can't think straight.

Exit that aisle, turn, take the next aisle back. Baby items. Know that can't be it. Stumble back to the main path. Avoid that woman with the shopping cart hurrying towards auto supplies. It stops me in my tracks long enough to make me look up. Staring across every aisle of the massive store. Do I recognize anyone here tonight, or is it morning now?

Security guard for the store is running past me, nods in my direction with a curt "sir" before hurrying along. Wait. Was that woman with the shopping cart wearing a shirt or even a bra?

Shake my head, and catch some odd detail on the floor. Purple. Dotted purple line going in a direction down an aisle. Follow that line, it may lead somewhere. Looks like someone splashed some paint onto a wheel and rolled it towards a destination. It might help.

Instead that purple dash leads to a crazy angry woman on an electric cart shouting at everything, especially the teenager walking beside her with a pained expression on his face. Think I know why. It's the smell from that woman. Good Lord. Flatulence like that would be enough to stun a half-sleeping doofus like me into coherence, if only to gain the awareness to run away.

Turn and run before that woman sees me and yells at me. Feel the urge to become a missing person in her presence. Move past the vacuum cleaners, head for the cheap furniture.

I stand in middle of the Knotts-Mart. Thinking. Trying to remember. Whose birthday is it?

Can't be my wife's. Dare not forget Jen's birthday. Can't forget it anyway, same day as Cinco De Mayo. I drove her crazy about it the four years I've known her and the two we've been married. She didn't mind first three years I kept taking her to Mexican restaurants to celebrate, but this year she made it damn clear she'd gotten sick of same menu. She wanted Italian instead.

Can't call her though. Jen is sleeping now, she'll be waking early for her flight back from the training conference in Boston. Could wait for when I know she'll head to the airport, but that's another three hours.

Walk down the main pathway, back towards housewares. Avoid that old woman. Stop in the kitchen supplies just to make sure I'm not seen. Who wants a frying pan for a birthday? If I buy it, better be for the friends I know who cook. That's just three. They have pans already. Not a good gift then.

Yawn. Turn and look down the rows of shelves towards the gleaming electronics section, the massive flat screens flashing ad after ad at me. Could always buy an electronics accessory that could cover all needs my friends would have. Unless they've already got it. Remember. Oh, right. There was a problem with getting Amy a Nook when she already owned three Kindles.

Swear I see a small cat running by me in the store. Do they have trained mousers to keep the store rodent-free? Nah. Falling back into sleep mode. Don't get distracted.

Someone knows. Out there, a friend is having a birthday, and my social circle should know.

Can't call anybody else. Might make the mistake of waking the friend I'm supposed to be shopping for. It will be a mistake to wake up all my friends at this time of night anyway.

Check smartphone. Oh, right, there might be a note. A message.

FUNNY LOCATIONS

The social media sites. Facebook. Someone should be posting about this by now. No. Damn, the wireless is down? Bad smartphone. Need new contract service. Should call the phone company first to complain.

Wait. There is someone I can call who'll be up this early or this late or whenever.

Bring up Joy on my contacts list and press Call. She'll be up. She's in India. That's the other side of the world from here. She'll know, we have the same circle of friends.

Joy's in a grumpy mood by the tone in her voice. "Why are you calling? Woke me from a nap, you know."

Ouch. I tell her the situation. I shake my head and cough, get my voice working. "I'm shopping for a birthday present for somebody, and I need to get a reminder whose day it is."

There's silence on the phone for about a minute. Maybe longer, so drowsy I can't tell time all that well.

Joy answers back, shouting at me over the phone. "You're an idiot. It's your birthday that's today, or tomorrow, however it is back there. Jesus. Happy birthday you crazy, and let me get back to sleep." Click.

Oh.

I buy myself a Lego set. The latest Millennium Falcon model with new radar dish. No one buys me Lego anymore. Do it for myself.

Wait for the line to disperse. Let that old woman depart on that cart and hope the store's ventilation system airs out the odor she leaves behind her. It takes an extra ten minutes but it's worth it. The cashier is a teenager nodding his approval at the box. "This looks incredible to put together. I take it this is a birthday present?"

Mutter a "Yesh." Smile as I buy this. Do feel good about this. Nobody buys me Lego anymore. Once that's done I can sleep the sleep of the just.

Except I got to go to the airport to pick up the wife. Oh right. She can help put the Lego Falcon together when we get home. Then we can sleep the sleep of the just.

JUST THROWING THIS OUT THERE

"This is not how I expected this evening to go."

"Are you okay doing this? If you want, we can go back."

"I got to admit, the party is a bit dull. I'm just worried we're stumbling about in the dark here."

"Keep the smartphone on then. Here, I've got my screen working as a flashlight. See?"

"Oh, that's clever."

"Just shine it towards the ground once in awhile. Make sure you're not tripping over anything."

"So what should I be looking for again?"

"It's hard to explain."

"Take the time to explain, then."

"I'm going to sound a little crazy saying it."

"I've seen you karate-chop a vampire last week. I get the feeling crazy is normal for you."

"That wasn't a kar... Ah, okay, let that go. Look, there was a thing that happened out here in the woods, okay, between the river and the house. Gary... lost something. He's claiming it's likely washed out to

FUNNY LOCATIONS

the bay, but he's been acting weird, and I've caught him messing with something yesterday that makes me think..."

"Which one's Gary?"

"The one with the tattooed third eye."

"I didn't see anybody with a third eye on their forehead."

"It's not on his forehead."

"...Well, okay, it's not like I've seen any of your buddies naked or anything..."

"It's not the issue at the moment though. We've got to find it. I've got the feeling Gary's hiding it from us."

"What should I be looking for?"

"Something metallic. The size of a shoebox."

"Where should I be looking then?"

"Somewhere on the ground, but hidden. Any pile of odd rocks, or logs. Look under the logs out here."

"What about that?"

"What's that? You find... what the hell is that?"

"Looks like a scorpion."

"THE SIZE OF A DOG!"

"Okay. Can you karate-chop that?"

"Run!"

"I'll take that as a no."

A WANDERING MUSE

Where does my Muse reside?

Right now, on the other side of the world.

And she's not answering her phone.

I look out the window of the shuttle service at the airport, the drab grey of late winter obscuring the Virginia landscape. Whatever impulse that's driven my Muse to seek better climes, I don't blame her.

I get one last call from my mom, hassling me from her winter condo in Boca, before I board the flight heading West. "Who's gonna clean your apartment while you're gone?" she asks. She knows there's a year's worth of dust already. What's two more weeks of it going to do?

My laptop's no good in the cramped seating of the plane. My tablet app works, so I make myself start a chapter. Any story will do.

I get as far as the first line. "This is how I want to wake up."

Nothing else comes to me as follow-up.

The tablet battery wears out before landing at San Francisco.

It takes an hour to wait for the connecting flight to Hong Kong. I find a charging station near the boarding gate, and spend the time flipping between the map app and the browser's online gallery of travelogue photos. Smiling people, crowded streets, distant mountains, everything inviting and everything unknown.

The battery is only half-charged by the time the plane pulls away from the gate. I decide to leave it alone, even though there's nothing else worth doing besides getting up once an hour to stretch my legs. The in-flight movie is another Air Bud sequel. *Why, God?*

Everything after landing is a blur. I observe the crowds as I go through the motions of surviving customs and security checks, recovering luggage, and arranging for a taxi to the hotel. I don't recognize any faces. This is my first time here. I wouldn't know anyone. If I were looking for a face in the crowd, this would make sense. But no one really catches my eye.

I lost count of the number of near-collisions my taxi driver gets us through. He's chattering through five different languages as he's speeding through every intersection. I pay him with a large tip, on the understanding (if any) that he not drive at all the next three weeks. I may be here two weeks but I don't want to feel responsible for the week *after* I leave.

Hotel check-in is much smoother. I'm greeted at the desk by a polite petite young woman, her blond hair framing a pixie face. "Will you be here long?" she asks, a hint of Shakespearean training in her accent.

"A couple of weeks," I reply as I fill out the paperwork. "Trying to find some inspiration."

The desk clerk keeps smiling. "Well, there are some spectacular mountain views and pathways you can walk. That might help you."

Walking about the hotel's neighborhood does perk my energy a bit. I feed off the buzz of activity, of people in motion, the scent of the restaurants and the noise of the crowds. I can't tell if my body is still on East Coast time but I do fall into bed late at night, closing my eyes to the neon glow of the city and finding much-needed sleep.

. . .

My muse kicks me in the head, brushing her shoulder-length auburn hair out of her face to glare at my slumbering form. "Wake up. Let's go."

She escorts me down the elevator as I'm making sure my pants are zipped. "I'm working an assignment already," she pauses to brush some lint off my shirt, "and we've got a busy day."

"That's nice to know," I mutter half-awake. "It'd be nicer to know what you're doing, and what name you're going by."

With a smile she hands me a red business card. Victoria Seun printed in white. Her email is *IWillPunchYou247 AT Sina dot com*. There is nothing else on it. "I am what you call a consultant on private issues. On occasion I fix those issues."

We walk past the complimentary breakfast bar. "We can get a coffee where we're going."

"And where are we going?" I ask her, trying not to bump my laptop case against the revolving door.

Victoria winks at me as we step outside, her sapphire eyes sparkling in the morning light. "Everywhere."

It turns out Victoria is part Chinese, British grandmothers on both her parents' sides, and while her family left during the Transition she came back because the pay was good and she had some family issues to resolve. Nothing to do with her current consulting work, which involved discrete shootouts at mountainside retreats along the Eight Immortals ridges, covert meetings with her ex-boyfriend Cong with the Security Bureau along the waterfalls of the Tai Yeun Stream, and a satisfying arrest at a Quarry Bay teahouse of a rogue Russian businessman who dies of radiation poisoning before he can make a plea deal.

I'm three novels into Victoria's assignments by the end of the first week. My muse is putting me through the paces, as I put to print every word of her cliffhanging non-stop action. Well, okay, some of the chapters go into the lavish dinners and steamy romantic encounters with dubious anti-heroic men – and one woman – Victoria hooks up with during her escapades. But hey, eating and sex count as action, right?

We run into that taxi driver three different times. Third time literally, well at least in the story I'm writing. Good thing every character's air bags deployed during that particular traffic jam, except for the bad guys who all keep forgetting to buckle up as well, anyway shame on them.

Victoria's guiding me through all these incredible places I keep spotting on the maps, I'm taking pictures of the prettier locales. I'm having fun following her up and down these streets more colorful in real life than on the Google pages.

I'm surprised there is enough of Hong Kong still standing by our second week here. At least in the pages of the drafts I've typed over the days. In my mind's eye I can see Victoria sword in hand standing in silhouette as the sun sets through the smashed office windows of that tall skyscraper right over there overlooking the bay. Oh, right. There's about fifty skyscrapers along the bay. I'm going to need to come up with a fictional name for it.

Three full novels ready for editing that second week, a fourth outlined with the end chapter already finished, but then Victoria turns to me halfway through the fifth novel rough draft. "You know something? There's a few things about what I've done in England that you've overlooked."

I glance at the website map glowing on my tablet. I see my muse moving along the streets of London, hurrying to another spot that matters to her. A family home perhaps, or a favorite bookstore. I use my fingers to pinch the tablet screen, stretching out the map to where I see more of the world I need to see.

Victoria's on that map somewhere, and she can inspire me further at that next stop.

I don't have a problem booking the next flight. So what if there's four more weeks of dust piling up back home?

MY LAST PRAYER

I'm driving along the lunar landscape of the Jersey industrial skyline, the turnpike still dark even as that sun rises like a red fireball on a new morning. I got a state trooper on my bumper, chasing me down with his red and blue party lights flashing in my rear view, even though I've stuck to the speed limit. Every man's brother gets pulled over by the traffic cops, I swear, even when we done no wrong. I ain't pulling over until I get home back where my baby is, I had my Wanda crying over the phone that she misses me just as I was getting off the night shift my boss put me on.

I got the radio playing, trying to find anything with a good backbeat, but at this time of morning in Jersey the radio's jammed up with gospel preachers yelling about Heaven and Hell, selling long distance salvation. I've had this one guy, you can hear the sweat from his brow dripping on the mic, on the car speakers shouting as though nobody can hear him, and after getting his phone number screamed into my ears for the fifth time in a row I decided "What the Hell, Lord" and dialed in to see if I could get a chance to speak my faith. I pressed those numbers into the cellphone sitting in the passenger seat, with a lady putting me on hold waiting my turn in line for the last two minutes.

I made sure the radio dialed down to avoid feedback when the salesman preacher starts shouting through my phone "And HERE NOW is a PILGRIM who says he's on the Jersey Turnpike OFFERING UP HIS PRAYERS TO OUR GOD AND SAVIOR and YOU are ON THE AIR NOW WHAT CAN YOU SAY TO THE FLOCK THIS MORNING."

I kept myself from shouting, I knew what I had to say. "Well Mister Gospel DJ person, here I am on the road, driving back from a job with a boss who hates me and with a cop car chasing me down for no reason at all, trying to get back to the girl who loves me since I met her on Scrap Metal Hill where she made my heart stand still, and all I wanna do is see if you wanna hear my last prayer."

I finally shout like he does, only with faith and resolve and love. "HEY HO ROCK AND ROLL DELIVER ME FROM NOWHERE!"

I hang up the phone and dial the radio up, catching the delay between here and there and back again. I smile as my last prayer makes it to the airwaves and I know the Good Lord is with me now.

The DJ preacher huffed into his microphone and shouted his angered rebuke. "YOU... YOU THINK THAT'S FUNNY JOKER? YOU MOCK GOD WITH THAT DEMON MUSIC. Well... Well this here my flock... THIS IS THE BLASPHEME of our FALLEN WORLD, these sick... LONG-HAIRED ATHEISTS who show contempt for us... US TRUE BELIEVERS trying to fight for GOD'S GLORY on Earth. And you know, for FIFTY DOLLARS TO OUR WEBSITE I CAN TELL YOU HOW TO PRAY... How to STRIKE DOWN OUR WRATH ON THESE HEATHENS WHO..."

The radio exploded with the sound of angels blowing all this into the sea, and then silence. I switched the dial to other stations, even the ones I don't like. All those radio waves and nothing on.

I glanced back at the cop car that had been chasing me along the

Turnpike. A couple seconds later he turns off the party lights and backs off, taking the third off-ramp and disappearing into the streets of Philadelphia.

It took me three hours to reach Freehold. Covered a lot of ground. I found Wanda curled up on the sofa, television on but the sound off. I knelt to wake her and whispered "Hey baby can I make you breakfast?"

Wanda opened up those big brown eyes of hers with a single tear down her cheek and she said, "Bruce, you should see the news on Channel 57. They're talking about how every gospel radio station got hit by lightning this morning. They had to call in all the emergency people even the highway patrolmen. What do you think happened?"

I grinned to let my baby know everything was going to be okay. "I think it means the Good Lord loves rock and roll."

Wanda touched my face and asked "Bruce, does that include Bon Jovi?"

I held Wanda gently in my arms and answered "Maybe."

THE LIBRARIAN

THE VOYNICH KEY

"So what are you doing in the Waldo Florida police station?"

The Librarian finished her question by adjusting the silver-rimmed reading glasses on her face. She didn't need to wear them any more than she needed to wear a trench coat in the summer, but this was part of her persona in this time and place of the late 20th Century. This was how Troy Viator viewed his fellow librarians in the field, and this was how she looked the last two times she worked with him.

Troy still as lanky as ever dangled his long arms between the cell bars, leaning forward with a guilty expression. "Well, I was in a bit of a rush to get back to Gainesville."

The Librarian nodded once. "You're still working at University of Florida?"

Troy grinned for a second. "Despite your disappointment, no the library hasn't fired me yet. Warren's got me helping him still with special acquisitions for the archives."

"Which I take was something you were working on when the cops caught you for speeding."

Troy couldn't grin at that. "Well, it's not like I ever got caught before..."

"Through the world's most infamous speed trap?" The Librarian pushed her glasses up as she pinched the bridge of her nose. "Jesus, Troy. Even small furry lifeforms from Alpha Centauri know about Waldo. Just how fast were you going?"

Troy shrugged and muttered a ridiculously high number.

The Librarian dropped her hand from her nose and glared at the imprisoned bibliographic specialist. "Troy, that's warp speed. You've lived in this part of Florida long enough to know not to... Ahh, forget it."

The Librarian turned with both arms raised. "I don't care now. Leave him to rot. I don't care why Warren called me in on this," she growled as she took her first steps out of the cell block.

"Wait!" Troy pressed against the bars, arms stretched as far as possible as he begged for help. "There's a reason, I swear! Go check my trench coat, check the pockets, some of my notes should still be in the pockets!"

The Librarian didn't glance back, but sighed as she tapped on the door. "Can I talk to the police chief?"

The chief was the one who opened the door back out to the cramped workspace of the police department. He stood as intimidating as possible: Taller than Troy, broad-shouldered, tanned and weathered face with a thin white mustache, clean unwrinkled uniform with a bright pocket badge showing off the name Williams. He glowered downward. "You ready to pay his bail?"

"Not just yet," The Librarian replied, pointing her finger in a direction past the chief. "You got his trench coat with my Satchel, right?"

Chief Williams stepped to one side, letting the Librarian pass him into the narrow walking space between cubicles. "He's been processed. Everything in his pockets was put aside for possible evidence."

FUNNY LOCATIONS

"Troy had notes, in one of his pockets. He said I needed to look at them."

The police chief glanced to a cubicle at the other end of the room. "Should be in one of the pouches then. The deputy who brought him in, his desk's over there. Let's go take a look."

The pouch with Viator's name inked on the label tag sat atop the pile on the deputy's desk, under the Librarian's Satchel that she had to surrender in order to visit the prisoner. Williams tapped the Librarian's hand as she reached towards the pile. "Ma'am, gonna ask you not to touch anything until we hand it to you, alright?"

He lifted the Satchel first to drop it to the floor, muttering "Bit heavy." He grabbed the pouch and flipped it open. "Wallet, keys, here we go." The chief pulled out a Ziploc bag with loose papers inside. "This what you need? I'm sorry, what was your name again?"

The Librarian blinked, remembering her identity within this time frame. "You can call me Kei," she replied. She mentally took note of who Kei was in this timeline, her Japanese-American appearance, her love of nonfiction and Elmore Leonard novels. She held up her right hand at the bag. "May I?"

"As long as you lay the notes out so we both can read what he's got," Williams answered. "I don't want any secret messages going in and out of my office."

"Fair deal."

The chief handed the Librarian the bag and allowed her to sort the papers as she pulled them out onto the work desk. She turned a few of the sheets upward, revealing handwritten notes scribbled atop what looked to be photocopies of book pages. "What the...?" The Librarian muttered to herself, taking a moment to identify the odd-scripted writing.

"What the hell language is that in?" Chief Williams asked as he leaned forward, pushing his shoulder against hers.

"It looks like Troy had made copies of a rare manuscript, an old folio if you can see how the pages themselves are..." The Librarian paused, stunned, and them stammered on. "This can't be it. That book is up at Yale. And I don't recognize these illustrations, they aren't plant life as they're supposed to..."

She flipped over to the next photocopy of another page. The second page didn't have Troy's notes on it, this one had someone else's, and in another ancient language.

"Now I'm not a college scholar or anything," Williams mentioned as he pointed a finger at the second page. "But that looks like one of them older European writings, like Latin."

"It's Greek," The Librarian whispered back. "Written underneath the original script, as though someone was translating..." Her eyes widened. "By the Gods."

She grabbed that sheet and ran back towards the cell block. She thudded against the door, turning the handle as hard as possible. "Can you let me back in there, chief?"

Williams pulled his identity card from its belt hook and swiped it across the wall lock next to the doorway. The Librarian tried the handle again and swung the door open, moving quickly to Troy's cell.

Troy had remained leaning against the bars, smiling again as the Librarian hurried toward him with the page up in her hand, shoving towards his smug face. "Tell me this isn't the Voynich Manuscript."

"It's not the manuscript," Troy grinned. "But it *is* the script. It matches up."

The Librarian's jaw dropped. "There's a *second* book? You found one?"

"Well, sort of," Troy's grin faded as he looked at the police chief waiting at the door. He leaned closer to her to whisper, "A collector had passed away, the estate had asked us for an evaluation of the man's shelves, I spotted the odd font, noticed the artwork was nothing like the original, realized what it was, and... Um, I made arrangements to bring it back here to Gainesville. And you noticed the Greek scribbles?"

The Librarian nodded. "Yes. Are they real?"

"They're not mine. I don't write in books. Someone else did, long time ago if the age of that ink fading out tells me anything. And you

FUNNY LOCATIONS

know me, I'm not a linguistics expert." Troy tapped the bars with his right hand. "But Warren is, he knows Hellenistic Greek, I'm pretty sure that's what the translation attempt was working with, and that's why I was in such a rush to get here."

"What are you all talking about?" Chief Williams interrupted.

The Librarian turned to him, holding up the photocopy. "The Voynich Manuscript is a rare book, written in a language no one's ever seen before, without any means of translating it. What Troy's found, a second book separate from the original, that alone would be a huge find."

She tapped at the page. "If this Greek translation of Voynich is correct, if it's working, then we've got a Rosetta Stone situation here. An actual Key to Voynich language. We're talking one of the greatest mysteries in encryption, in all of bibliographic history could get resolved."

She returned her attention to Troy. "You've got the second manuscript with you?"

Troy glanced at the Waldo police chief and then nodded at the Librarian. "I didn't see the cops search the whole car, they've just brought me in for being an asshole on the highway. It should be wrapped up in the suede cloth in the back seat."

The Librarian turned around with an eager grin on her face. "Chief Williams, can I go get that book from his car?"

The police chief took a moment to think it over. "Well, he's only in here for the excessive speeding, and now I'm a bit curious myself about this Voyneech stuff you're talking about. So let's go take a look."

Two minutes later the Librarian and the police chief were standing in the station's impound lot.

"Where the hell is his car?" Chief Williams shouted.

It wasn't an auto shop as much as it was an open field littered with cars in varying degrees of rust and age. They were at least lined up in rows making it easy for the police officers to approach the tent at the far end of the yard where loud drilling could be heard.

Chief Williams approached the pair of legs underneath a dinged-up Chevy SUV, bending at his knees just enough to reach down and grab the oil-stained work boots by both ankles to yank the mechanic out with one strong pull. The mechanic screamed for a second, then yelled "Watch it you moron I'm working here!"

Chief Williams glared at the mechanic. "Donald, you just have to be the stupidest carjacker in the whole state of Florida. That takes some doing, don't it?"

Donald the mechanic took a minute to blink a couple of times while looking at the small crowd assembled around him. Not only at the two Waldo police deputies standing at a distance to help ensure the mechanic won't run for it, but he stared at the two trench coat wearing academians standing close to the police chief staring back at him in mild annoyance.

"Oh, hey," Donald finally replied, dropping the power drill in his hand to the ground before wiping both hands on an already stained-covered work shirt. "Chief, didn't hear you coming round. What's all this about a carjack?"

Chief Williams swung his foot out to kick the power drill a good distance away. "I had me a speeder brought in with his rental car put into impound, only it's not there anymore. You're the only one in Alachua County with both a rap sheet for auto theft *and* with a cousin working in my department, so you do the math."

The Chief kept glaring at Donald while pointing a thumb over his shoulder. "I had to let this moron out of the jail cell so I could put your cousin in there instead. I had to forgive his speeding ticket because, God help us, you're dumber than he is."

Troy rose a hand, mouth opening to issue a protest, but the Librarian reached over and gently pushed his hand down while shaking her head.

Williams lowered himself, putting one knee on Donald's chest,

FUNNY LOCATIONS

making the mechanic gasp in pain. "I don't see the car in your yard, Donnie. What happened, you already sold it off?"

"I don't know what..." Donald started to defend himself but Williams knelt down harder on his chest, causing the mechanic to wheeze. "Help me, stop this... ahhh. I'll talk! Get... gasp... up!"

Williams lifted his body just enough to give Donald some fresh air to inhale. "Talk."

The mechanic groaned and thumped his head into the dirt. "Okay, look, it was a new car, rentals are insured right, it was something good to strip for parts, that's all that happened and..."

Williams lowered his body, pressing the knee again. "It takes a crew to strip a car that fast, and where did the parts go? You're gonna name names, Donnie, before I'm done with you and your..."

"Um, Chief?" The Librarian interrupted as she stepped towards one side of the interrogation taking place. "I know the chop shop thing is a big deal, but I'm worried about the item we're looking for."

Williams didn't look at her, but raised himself to where his knee was no longer on Donald's chest. "You're gonna answer this lady's questions, boy, and then we'll get back to business, understand? Answer her truthfully or I'm gonna drag out my questions a lot longer than you think."

The Librarian shrugged at Donald before asking. "When you stripped the car down, there was luggage still in the car. Personal items. There was a book, in a carrying box wrapped in..."

"Oh yeah, all that stuff, yeah," Donald nodded quickly. "Uh, there wasn't much else in the car but that box, it was a weird looking book. Written in German or something, all the pictures looked like witchcraft stuff so..." The mechanic paused as he glanced at Williams. "Uh, I made the call to sell that thing off, good money for a spell book right?"

"You sold it? Already?" The Librarian knelt down. "To whom?"

"I can already guess," Williams answered. "Her name's Charlene, but she..." He sighed and shook his head. "She calls herself Checksha or something. She's the one at the weekend flea market selling dragon candlesticks. She'd be selling more... obscene stuff but we talked her down from that after a few complaints from the locals."

The Librarian glanced towards Troy. "Which day is this?"

"Excuse me?" Williams raised a hand in her direction. "You don't know which day this is?"

The Librarian took a moment to look away, pursing her lips, trying to figure out a reasonable explanation about how her temporal-spatial jaunts make her look track of actual time. She heard Troy speak up. "It's been a stressful morning, Kei probably had to fly down here before getting her bearings and all."

She turned in his direction, noticing an odd expression on Troy's face as he continued talking. "Today's Thursday. Flea market's closed about now, it's only a weekend thing right?"

"She's still in high school if I recall her age last time I had to deal with her," Williams half-growled, half-sighed. "So she's not in school either. Odds are she's at her grandma's house, out in the woods between here and Orange Heights."

The police chief knelt again to press his knee on Donnie's chest. "I'll get you the address so you can follow up with her. I'm gonna finish up business here."

"You know, in all the times we've worked together," Troy spoke as the two librarians walked down a dirt driveway, the ground worn down at the tire paths, "I don't think you've ever mentioned where it is you really come from. I mean, I do think about it once in awhile, we just reach out with an email or a phone call and then... boom, you show up. Even if it's supposed to be out in California, or somewhere west, you're here faster than you should."

The Librarian was walking on one dirt lane while Troy walked on the other. She didn't look at him, instead staring forward at the shape of a two-story house starting to appear through the trees ahead of them. "It was never really something I can talk about."

"Well it's just this time you said the word 'when' that caught my

FUNNY LOCATIONS

attention. Being someone in the here and now, that's one thing. But you're talking like you're more than that. You've mentioned other things before when you've helped out that..." Troy stopped walking, waiting for the Librarian to stop as well and turn to him for the next part of the conversation. "If you can tell me this much. Are you someone who can just... jump from time past and time future as well as just being here at our beck and call?"

"I'm just a Librarian, same as you." She noticed Troy's skeptical stare, and took a moment to let her Satchel slide from her shoulder to land softly in the grass between tire paths. She raised a hand to her face, pointing with her index finger. "This face, the one you know, it's not always the face I wear. This trench coat I'm wearing, even in the sweltering Florida sun, it's a reflection of you, of what you tend to wear when you're on these quests of yours. I take this woman's form and appearance because it's your expectation of I what I should look like."

She reached up with that hand to wiggle her glasses for a second. "I don't even need to wear glasses, it's just part of the perception you have. The only things constant about me are that I know a lot of things to help me research, to help me help you." She then pointed down at the Satchel. "And this. My tool kit of sorts."

"Your Bag of Infinite Holding, I'd guess," Troy smirked.

"Something like that, yes." The Librarian reached down to reclaim her Satchel, sliding it back up to her shoulder. "Everything else is an illusion. The only facts are the ones we're hunting down."

She turned to keep walking towards the house. "The easiest way I can explain myself. I have been everywhere and anywhere. I will be, eventually. I can't explain it any other way than to say that as long as there's been a Library there has always been a Librarian."

Troy hurried his steps to match the Librarian's pace towards their destination. "Alright. That is a valid answer. It's good to know."

"And knowing is half the battle," The Librarian chuckled back, which got Troy laughing as well.

They were still in high spirits as they cleared the wooded path to get into the clearing surrounding a well-kept but aging Victorian-style house. They were at least a safe enough distance away from that house when it exploded.

It still took a few minutes for both Troy and the Librarian to stagger to their feet, stumbling more than once recovering from the shock of getting knocked backward from the explosion. The Librarian's ears were ringing, her other senses still stunned and shuddering with an adrenaline rush. Troy shouted something but she couldn't hear it. "What?"

"I said," Troy kept shouting, "This is the third house that's blown up on me!"

"What?"

"I said I'm getting sick and tired of houses blowing... Ahhh, let's just wait until the medics arrive!" Troy patted his trench coat pocket to pull out his smartphone. "Hopefully by the time they get here our ears will stop ringing!"

One ambulance, three fire trucks, and five police cars later, Williams approached the two bibliographic specialists as they were getting examined by the EMT crew for splinters and other signs of damage.

"So there I was, rounding up a chop shop out towards the Gainesville Speedway when I get a call that we got a house blowing up out along Highway 301." The police chief glared at both Troy and The Librarian. "So now I'm thinking this speeding ticket just literally went from a nothing-burger to a Murder One, except for the fact I knew Charlene's grandmother worked at the Dollar General so I called there to make sure she was okay, and then it's just a question of whether the teenage goth girl wasn't killed."

Williams pulled his sunglasses off, wiping one frame with his tie. "Just spoke with the fire chief, he's letting me know there's no sign of a body inside, just half the second floor blown away and the rest of the home too charred to get rebuilt. Now I've got to find out why I got a couple of crazy librarians causing all this property damage over an old book in a weird language."

"That is something I would like to know as well," The Librarian replied. She rubbed at the bandage stuck to her forehead and turned her attention to Troy. "I was not aware that there would be other parties chasing after a Voynich manuscript."

Troy glanced between The Librarian and the police chief. "Oh."

"You said you'd recovered the book from a private collector who had passed away recently," The Librarian continued. "It would be nice to know how that person really died and what the circumstances were that allowed you to claim the book."

Troy grimaced for a second, then nodded. "Got the call from the collector's estate up in Ohio well after he'd died, the guy's daughter was getting pressure from somebody who was creeping her out. She preferred passing the guy's personal library to his alma mater, so I head up, begin evaluating the books. Most of them were first edition fictions, no problem."

"Come across a shelf panel with this symbol for Mercury." Troy glanced at the police chief. "It's from alchemy, the symbol represents the mind. I check it, there's a false panel to that shelf, and that's where this one book was stashed."

"So this collector knew what he had was important?" The Librarian asked.

"Yeah, Kei, and the second I saw the script I knew it too." Troy did a waving motion with his left hand. "I'm halfway through copying every page with the handheld scanner to my laptop when the creepy buyer arrives at the house. The daughter delays him at the door while I shove the book back into the hiding shelf, but next thing that happens is the creep threatens the both of us with slow poisonous deaths if we didn't give up the whole collection to him."

"Describe him." The Librarian said it as an order than a request.

Troy closed his eyes to focus on the memory. "About an inch or two shorter than me. Narrow face. Blond hair but black goatee. Neck tattoo wrapping behind both ears but didn't get a good look." He opened his eyes. "Dressed in steampunk outfit, purple coat with white flourish on the lapels."

The Librarian took a minute in thought to review her suspects. "Doesn't narrow it enough. I know too many occultists and alchemists within this time frame who fit that description. He never left a name?"

"He didn't stay long enough." Troy smirked for a moment. "When he threatened me I gave him the Diogenes Club greeting of *I Too Am From Arcadia*, and that scared him enough to turn and walk for the front door."

"So you got out of there with the book first chance you got." The Librarian smiled back for a second before scowling. "But it seems like he'd figured out how to follow you to here."

"How did he know where Charlene would be before we got here?" Troy asked.

"If he followed us to Donnie's yard, he got a head start on us dropping you off in front of the driveway," Williams spoke up, glancing about the woods surrounding the half-destroyed home. "Parked out there somewhere to sneak up, maybe tried setting a trap for you when he found no one here."

"Not a good trap if he did that," Troy answered, standing up from the ambulance bumper and turning around to search the woods as well. "Went off before we even got close enough to get charred."

"I doubt it was meant to be a trap," The Librarian suggested. "Men like that don't handle frustration all that well."

"Hopefully that means he didn't get Charlene or the manuscript," Troy replied. "If she wasn't here, it's a question now about where she could be."

"Should be no question at all." The Librarian stood up from where she sat and approached Chief Williams. "Take us to the flea market. It's the only other place she could have gone."

· · ·

FUNNY LOCATIONS

Charlene's candle store sat some distance from the market pavilions: A shed painted with blue and yellow starbursts, and a green dragon tail wrapping around the edge of the roof. A simple sign above the doorway invited everyone into "Wyvern's Wicks" although at that moment the door was closed.

"Time to knock and be polite about it," The Librarian muttered as she rapped twice on the door.

No one answered.

Troy strolled to the right side of the shed. "You've got perfectly good windows," he shouted, "we can see you in there!"

"What's she doing?" Williams asked as he stood a few steps distant, one hand resting on his holstered gun.

Troy turned his head back and forth examining the interior. "She's putting down a chalk circle with wards and what looks like Celtic symbols. Couple of candles lit on the floor as well."

The Librarian turned the door handle. "All of her preparations to protect herself from evil spirits, and she forgets to lock the front door."

The door opened outward, so The Librarian swung it wide and propped it with an upturned flower vase from nearby. She looked into the shed, noting the shelves mounted into the walls decorated with various metal-cast figures of fantasy creatures from dragons to lycanthropes. A chair sat askew in a corner. As Troy described, a large uneven chalk circle covered most of the floor, a magic defense for anything coming. In the middle of that circle knelt a petite turquoise-hair girl, holding up a large leather-bound book with a wine-colored cover as she whispered some mantra for protection.

The Librarian examined the magic circle. "You've gotten the four candles placed properly," she hinted with a smile, "but your astral symbols are in the wrong order."

The girl stopped whispering. "Really?" she asked.

"Actually it's been awhile since I made one of these, so I could be wrong." The Librarian bent down to pinch the flame of the candle nearest to her long coat. "Gonna put this out before I catch on fire."

123

She stood upright and stared right at the teen's green eyes. "What name do you go by?"

Charlene blinked once, realizing that this intruder to her shack would accept her by her chosen name. "They call me Cypris. It's my Wiccan name. What name do you go by?"

"Around here, they call me Kei," she stepped over the line, respecting not to disturb the chalk. "But my true name is the Librarian."

Cypris stood up, keeping eye contact with her. "True names have power."

The Librarian grinned. "Not always, from what I've learned. True names have *meaning*."

The teen broke eye contact, lowering her head. "You're here for the grimoire?"

"Yes, but it may not be a grimoire. The language remains unknown. Have you heard of the Voynich Manuscript up at Yale?"

Cypris glanced up quickly, a smile on her face. "Is this a copy?"

"It may be a sister book." The Librarian held out her hand. "May I see it?"

"No," a deep male voice spoke from outside the shed, "she may not."

Everyone turned towards the approaching man, who wore a narrow face with blond hair and black goatee. The Librarian spotted the edges of the neck tattoo wrapping behind both the man's ears and recognized one being a planetary symbol.

"Yup." Troy noted as he took a step back. "It's the creepy guy."

Williams growled a "Hold it" at the man while keeping his hand on his holstered gun. The man paused in mid-stride, quietly posing himself attentively waiting for the next move.

The Librarian shook her head. "I know you. We've met before. Paracelsus Velmont, as you would like to be called. Although your father called you Joseph, if I recall."

The man's expression turned into a dark sneer for just a moment before he returned to a placid veneer. "I don't think we've met. I would remember your face. Unless you're one of those who... change with the times."

"Oh, I change from time to time," The Librarian nodded. "We met in Philadelphia. It was regarding a certain artifact from ancient Sumer."

The man's eyes widened, and he returned the nod. "You have changed. Ah, I recognize your Satchel now. I remember, you were a Librarian back then. Very well. You can call me Velmont, that should keep things... civilized."

"Blowing up houses is civilized?" Troy quipped.

Velmont glared at Troy for longer than just a moment. "Keeping me from my rightful property is uncivilized, if not outright theft. I do hope the tome is in this location right now, so I may claim it."

"Police Chief Williams," The Librarian paused as she gestured one hand towards Velmont, "let me introduce you to a modern-day alchemist. You can spot them by the smug bearing, the various chemical odors they carry with him, as well as displaying a fashion sense that's worse than Troy's."

"HEY!"

"Why are you here, Velmont." The Librarian turned away from Cypris and the manuscript, stepping into the doorway to block the entrance against the alchemist. She reached her left hand into her Satchel, feeling for the small vials stored in a particular corner for safekeeping. She knew she needed a reasonable threat to hold him back. "Last we met you weren't dealing in old books, you were trading off your grandfather's reputation with..."

"I am not here for reminiscing, Librarian," the alchemist interrupted. "I am here for my property, wrongfully stolen by your companion in the trench coat here."

Velmont stepped with calm purpose towards the police chief. "Officer, let me present the receipt for my rare manuscript, rightfully purchased from the previous owner not some three days ago."

"That's a lie," Troy barked at him, but the alchemist ignored him as he handed the paper to Williams.

The police chief took the slip of paper and read it, holding it close at the lower half of the slip for inspection. "Well, my thinking is that you've got a bill here alright." He glanced at Velmont before holding the paper towards the Librarian. "I may need the lab boys to make sure, but for what I know this isn't signed with an ink pen. Whole thing's laser printed."

The Librarian lifted up her glasses with her right hand, opening her eyes wide and letting her perception expand. She could feel her inner light shining outward from her vision, letting her truly *See* all that she needed. In that moment of illumination, she examined not just the text and signatures on the paper but the paper itself. She could see where the fraud was not so subtle.

She blinked as her eyes returned to a relaxed state. Williams stared back at her with some awe, having witnessed part of her supernatural ability. "Lady, what the hell did you just do?"

"I made certain that receipt's not real," The Librarian smiled as she turned her attention from the police chief towards the now-enraged alchemist. "I'm not impressed that you relied on creating a fake document, and in such a cheap way. Using a computer and a Hewlett Packard printer. Tsk. I would have thought a man with your talents could have forged documents with a little more flair. Shame."

Velmont began to open his purple coat, reaching his right hand towards an inner pocket. "If you think you can stop..."

"Let me interrupt you this time." The Librarian moved faster with her left hand grabbing at a glass vial and raising it out of her Satchel. "I'm holding here a fancy little compound. Wonderful little liquid inside it. All I have to do is throw it on you, make sure I hit your skin..."

"And then I will burst into flames? Or some other such ridiculousness?" Velmont mocked. "Please. I'm an expert in such things. There's no singular mixture that can do that, not with a bottle that size..."

"It won't work right away," The Librarian continued. "Because it's a binary agent."

Velmont's sneer changed to an expression of concern. He kept his right hand inside his coat but took a step back.

"It combines with any number of elements you alchemists love to use." The Librarian took a step forward, moving towards Troy. "Can't tell you which ones, because then you'll have to wonder how it will react to anything you've got back in your lab. Think carefully. It can mix with something as common as tin as a slow poison or a quick death. What's the most common liquid you've got, acetic acids? Maybe it works with that. It can mix with any of the gases your experiments generate. This gets into your blood, your sweat, your tears. And this stays in your system for about a year."

She handed the vial to Troy without taking her eyes off Velmont. "Think you can protect yourself from exposure, that you can hold off working in your lab? That you can go *anywhere* safely without triggering the binary? You might not even make it safely back to your car. Troy? Keep him honest. I've got some reading to do. I'm going to learn what we really have here before it gets messy."

The Librarian turned and walked back into the candle shack. She nodded to Cypris with both hands reaching towards the manuscript. "I need to see it, every page."

"You can translate this?" The teen Wiccan whispered.

"Not yet. I need to find out if someone else was properly translating it already." She removed the glasses from her head. "Hold these. I don't need glasses to truly See."

The Librarian placed the ancient tome atop Cypris's glass counter. She carefully opened the book to the first page, spotting the Greek text the unknown translator had scribbled onto the vellum. This she could read, from the years of experience living in the Hellenistic era itself.

"It's a biography of the person who had this back in the day," The Librarian spoke aloud, letting even Velmont know what she was discovering. "He's a student who was traveling Europe, recovered this book from Salzburg in 1803 when the city was facing invasion. Had to be the Napoleonic wars. He writes here that he had shown this book to professors who thought it a hoax, but he notes the illustrations and organization of the pages is too realistic to ignore."

She flipped the pages to where the actual text began. She took a minute to admire the illustration that greeted her, an elaborate drawing of silver-colored bricks interlocking to form a road and bridge, with a pair of winged angels walking across the path. She returned her attention to the Voynich handwriting and more important the Greek being used to translate. "Here we go. The student has the words detailing an introduction to... wait."

The Librarian blinked. "No, those letters don't match up."

She widened her eyes again, unleashing her ability to *See* all she could. Within a heartbeat the Librarian flipped one page after another, perceiving not the Voynich language but the growing failure of the Greek words turning into gibberish. She felt a twinge of disappointment, realizing the student was forcing words to fit into a pattern of script that didn't match from page to page.

She felt despair that the language remained a mystery even to herself. But as she sped through the entire volume, she also examined in detail the illustrations that illuminated every other page. What she saw in the patterns emerging from the drawings terrified her.

When the Librarian closed the book she closed her eyes, adjusting back to the reality of now. She turned to Cypris, who was just beginning to blink from watching the Librarian speed read the ancient book. "What just happened?"

"Enlightenment of a sort," The Librarian answered. She reopened the manuscript to a set of pages without illustrations, and turned to walk outside, lifting the book in front of her towards Velmont. "I want an honest answer out of you."

The alchemist glared at her. "Like you would believe me if I did?"

"If only to make sure you're honest to yourself." She lifted the book closer to his face. "Tell me, can *you* translate this?"

Velmont leaned forward, reading and blinking and then scowling. "Well, I have already read through the copy of the original Voynich to understand what could be gleaned from it."

FUNNY LOCATIONS

"But did you ever translate any of it? *Any* of this?"

"Oh no." Troy muttered nearby, and the Librarian noticed he was lowering the vial. "The translation's not working?"

"The translator was an *idiot*," The Librarian growled. "He was forcing the text to fit a narrative he already had. He was getting off track with his decoding by the second page."

Troy groaned. "All that effort, whole thing... Ah hell."

Velmont reached out with his right hand for the manuscript. "If it's all a worthless endeavor on your part..."

The Librarian closed the book and turned away, keeping him from touching it. "It's worthless for you. Without a way to translate it, there's no alchemy you can glean from this. As a rare book this still has value to us, and if you would so kindly leave us and this book alone it would be worth it for you to do so."

Velmont moved one leg forward. His face displayed no intention to walk away empty handed.

"I've still got the binary agent, guy." Troy warned. "And you're easy to hit from this range now."

The alchemist stopped his forward motion, stood upright, moved his legs back. He kept facing everyone else until he was a good distance away. "This business," Velmont did his best to sound intimidating, "is far from over, Librarian."

"The hell it isn't over!" Williams moved to keep pace with the retreating alchemist. "I've got this madman on an arson charge!"

"Let him go, chief," The Librarian answered. "You won't find anything to arrest him on. Like I said, I know Velmont. He's smart enough to avoid leaving any evidence of bombing that house." She paused and realized something. "Just like he did a good job hiding the evidence he poisoned that book collector he'd been trying to steal from. Am I wrong?"

Velmont glanced at Williams then back at The Librarian, and scowled a quiet threat in her direction. Then he turned around and ran.

"I don't care if you think I can't hold him. Dammit!" Williams gave chase as Velmont scurried into the maze of flea market pavilions.

The Librarian felt a hand on her elbow, and looked over her shoulder at Cypris standing there with a stunned expression. "Wait a minute. What happened to the... Did that creepy guy burn down my gran's house?"

The Librarian grimaced. "He... might have blown up half of it."

Cypris shuddered, tears forming. "No no no, my Gran was there when I left."

"Relax, she's fine. Police chief made sure she was at work," The Librarian smiled to calm the teen down.

The Wiccan girl kept shivering in fear. "But the house. Is it safe to...? If it's blown up what's going to happen to us?"

The Librarian handed the manuscript to Troy for him to hold, then reached back into her Satchel for a pencil and notepad. She scribbled some information and phone numbers onto a sheet. "Here. There should be emergency shelter for a day or three, this other number is to a federal housing grant I know that your grandmother can use to secure some money to rebuild. It'll be a tough few months for you, but I'll check back in with you to make sure you're all okay."

She tore the sheet from the notepad and handed it to Cypris, who stopped shivering but was sniffling back tears. "Oh it's... this is going to be so weird and all. And... oh no, my manga collection is gone..."

The Librarian turned and shoved an elbow into Troy's side. He grunted and muttered a soft "What?" before noticing that she was glaring at him. He kept whispering "What are you looking at me for?"

"It's partly your fault you dragged Velmont to Waldo in the first place," The Librarian hissed.

Troy's face went through a series of thoughtful wrinkles before he sighed and nodded. Speaking in Cypris' direction he grunted, "Okay, I will help rebuild your magna collection when your home gets rebuilt."

Another elbow into his ribs. "Fine," he added, "I will increase the collection double... Ow, okay, triple fold. Are we good then?"

"Not exactly," The Librarian noted, staring off into the direction

FUNNY LOCATIONS

of tires squealing at the start of a likely car chase to the county line. "I think the chief left us here without a ride."

"Well, I can... sniff, I can help you there," Cypris answered, wiping away the tears from her cheeks. "But can you help me clean up a bit here?"

"Not a problem," Troy replied. "Anything to stop Kei here from punching my ribs. Ow! Stop it..."

Putting out the candles and sweeping up the chalk took little time. Once the little store had returned to a semblance of normal, the Librarian reached out a hand to Troy who was standing nearest the manuscript, which had been safely put on the top shelf for safekeeping.

"Ah, that. All the trouble for this book, and it's going to end up on display as a curiosity," Troy sighed, handing it over to the Librarian. "At least it kept its secrets."

"Not entirely," the Librarian replied. She placed the book atop Cypris' store counter. "The language itself remains a secret, but I noticed a pattern in the artwork."

She opened the book, turning the pages until she got to a particular one late in the volume. "The first Voynich was filled with plant imagery, which made it seem like an herbal guide of sorts except that those plants didn't match anything in real life. There's been theories that the script is useless, but that the real secrets were hidden in those illustrations. Well, this second manuscript doesn't have plants, it has buildings, bridges, architecture, and... doors."

Troy looked down at the page that she was displaying as her example. He moved a little to get his head to turn the right direction. "Wait a minute, I think I've seen that diagram before..."

"It's incomplete, unless you match it to several other illustrations throughout the book. Put those diagrams together and you get a true illustration. Like a binary agent." The Librarian grinned at that irony.

"Speaking of which," Troy whispered as he pulled the small vial out of his trench coat pocket to hand back to her. "What was this, really?"

"My hair conditioner, silly." The Librarian smirked as she put the vial back into her Satchel. "I always carry a travel kit in case I have to stay over somewhere."

Troy smirked back and looked again at the illustration. "I'm not that big a researcher into advanced physics, but is this drawing detailing a gateway to a higher dimension?"

"It might be. And if this book was written in the same era as the first manuscript, it means we had someone thinking in multidimensional mathematics 300 years before anyone else." The Librarian stopped smirking. "If I had enough time to research it myself to make certain, along with working out a better key for the script."

"I guess so," Troy sighed as he nodded. "Good thing I'm going to tell Warren it ended up in safer hands. If Velmont was after it for just the unsolved writings, just think about who'll be after it if those illustrations went public."

"Thank you." The Librarian turned to the teen Wiccan who was standing on the other side of the counter, eyes wide from listening in on the dialog between the two. "Cypris, do you have the carrying box this manuscript was in?"

The teen nodded and reached under the counter, pulling out the carry case lined with protective cloth. The Librarian sorted out the cloth and slid the second Voynich manuscript into place, closing the lid.

She placed her Satchel on the countertop. The carrying box seemed larger than the Satchel, but the Librarian lowered the secured manuscript inside it as though there was room to spare.

Troy noticed the stunned expression on Cypris' face. "Oh, that's nothing. That Satchel of hers can fit an entire shelf of James Patterson novels."

"As if I'd ever stoop that low," The Librarian chuckled. "Although I did have trouble getting a Norman Mailer book to fit in there."

"All this librarian stuff you're throwing at me is insane," Cypris gasped. She blinked twice and asked, "Are you all hiring?"

THE GIRL WITH ANGEL WINGS

Jenny did not know how long she had been standing there in the women's restroom. Her mind was a blur from that moment she saw her husband Kevin sitting at that restaurant table – their table at Felicione's that they always reserved once a month, the one overlooking the Manhattan skyline, in an intimate corner meant for themselves – with this giggling young woman whose shoulders Kevin playfully kneaded as the two sat side by side.

Between the deep gasping sobs, Jenny felt the wetness across her face, her cheeks covered with tears. She realized she was doing something with her hands, and with a detached awareness she noticed herself furiously pulling at the wedding ring that no longer deserved to be on her finger.

How long had this been happening, Jenny raged to herself. *In their nine years of marriage, what the hell was Kevin doing behind her back?* How foolish could he be bringing *that girl* to this restaurant, risking the chance that his wife could come in on a long lunch with her investment firm partners to clinch a million-dollar deal with the client they invited?

Jenny bent over and tried to scream, but no sound came out. That business deal, what the hell was going to happen? She realized she had abandoned her colleagues at the maître d's booth the second she spotted her husband. The firm and the client had to be still there, confused by her fleeing the scene. Was it all ruined now?

Jenny yanked that ring at last off her finger. With a silent yell she tossed it blindly towards the sink counter, not caring as the ring clanged against marble and ceramic. Part of her hoped it would disappear down a drain. It was all ruined, her marriage, her work, her place in the world. She was stuck here in the ladies' room, falling apart along with everything else, falling like her tears.

A knock at the door caught her attention. *Why would anyone knock for the bathroom?* She worried it was one of her coworkers. She didn't want to be seen, not like this, it would hurt even more.

The door swung open, short heels clacking on the tile. Jenny's eyes widened, but she had no idea where to hide, especially from this person.

The young woman from Kevin's table stared back at her. She had taken off the colorful jacket she had at the table, revealing smooth tan shoulders in that spaghetti strapped blouse she wore. The pixie haircut did nothing to hide that shocking red color and accentuated those ocean blue eyes of hers, making her more girlish and tempting than anything Jenny saw in herself.

This girl stared back at her, not fear or judgment but curiosity. She let the restroom door close behind her as she stepped to the counter, dropping her hand purse to the counter. After a quick wash of her hands, the young woman stared at Jenny's reflection. "Can't have someone going through a worse lunch than me," she sighed.

The other woman turned and stood facing Jenny, and smiled as though a friend. "Lemme see your hands."

"What?" Jenny was stunned by the request.

The girl kept smiling as she reached out and took Jenny's hands by her fingers. The young thing raised them close to her vision. Her smile turned into a smirk. "No ring. Guess it's an idiot who failed to show up for a lunch date, huh."

FUNNY LOCATIONS

Jenny was not sure where this was going. She took a second to glance over at the sinks, wondering where she threw that ring away, and then looked back hoping she wouldn't get caught. "I'm sorry?"

The girl sighed. "Tears like that, it's some idiot breaking up with you. Shame on him though. I mean, look at you." She let go of Jenny's hands, began rubbing the older woman's arms, and stared right into her eyes. "You're tall, long-haired brunette with a sweet face and piercing green eyes. Even with that business armor you got on, I can tell you've got the breasts of a swimsuit model and the legs of a dancer. You're an Irish beauty, and any jerk leaving you hanging like this is an ass."

The young woman turned around to walk back to the counter. Jenny noticed then the young woman had tattoos, long white wings across her shoulder blades.

"Get over here with me," the woman requested, and Jenny with an uncertain step obliged. The girl pulled out a hand towel and wiped at Jenny's face with a gentle touch, cleaning away the running mascara that documented each fallen tear. She then wrapped an arm around the older woman.

"Repeat after me," the young woman instructed, staring straight towards the bathroom mirror. "I want to hear you say 'I am a pretty princess.'"

Jenny turned to glare down at her, but the girl kept staring at their reflections and she squeezed Jenny's arm for encouragement. "Trust me, you need this."

Jenny caught herself rolling her eyes in her reflection, but sighed. "Fine. I am a pretty princess."

"Good. Now say 'I am a pretty princess who deserves all the pretty ponies.'"

Jenny blinked at her mirror self for a second. "Pretty ponies?" She turned again but this time perplexed. "But I'm allergic to horses."

"Oh." The young woman scowled for once, but the smile returned as she glanced away from the mirror to stare up at Jenny. "What about a motorcycle?"

135

Jenny couldn't stop herself from giggling.

The young woman smiled even wider. "There, you see? Just needed to get a good laugh out of you. Seriously, the guy you're crying over is not worth it. They never are. I learned that lesson already."

Jenny looked at her with concern for once. "Already? How old are you?"

"Ehh, I'm 20." The girl shrugged while paying attention to her reflection, using her hands to smooth out her short hair and general appearance. "But I have this bad habit of dating older guys, like this jerk I'm with now."

The young woman let out a long sigh. Planting both hands on the counter, she leaned forward. "Thing is I came in here to get some fortitude, steel myself, you know. I gotta break it up with him. I mean sure I've been dating this guy the last couple months, but I swear he's lying to me about, well everything."

She glanced at Jenny, no tears in her eyes but every sign of regret. "I figured out the apartment he's been meeting me is owned by a company, lent out and stuff. It's not his real place. He's got to be cheating on me. Probably got a wife I don't know about, cheating on *her*, the bastard."

The young woman laughed, reaching over to touch Jenny's hand. "Hey, you should come watch. When I get back to our table, I'm just gonna say it to his face, might as well do it now, and walk away. That ought to cheer you up, watching that liar get dumped in public."

The young woman reached about the counter to her purse. She opened it and pulled out a business card. "Here," she offered.

Jenny took a decorative card of fantasy figures and superheroes. She flipped it over to see the name Sherry Rose and contact information.

Sherry smiled and leaned in. "I do artwork and photography from the comic book store I work at. I want you to call, get in touch with me." The young woman leaned in closer. "I really do want to see you,

FUNNY LOCATIONS

get you to model for me." She ended the suggestion with a quick kiss to Jenny's cheek.

Sherry turned away with an impish grin, her shoulder wing tattoos wiggling as she exited the ladies' room.

Jenny could only stand there with the woman's business card in her hand, her emotions shifting from shock to pity. "Oh, Sherry," she finally muttered, one last tear forming in Jenny's eye, "You didn't know."

AUTHOR'S NOTES

In a previous story collection I had published, I included author's notes because I'd like the readers to understand – hopefully – where my story ideas are coming from and how the writing process works (sort of). With this anthology, I'd like to keep that going.

Some of these stories originally appeared in that anthology, which was – Good Lord – 20 years ago and in some ways lost in the eddies of time. I recovered the ones I felt were my best works of that earlier era, adding them into this collection with the more recent efforts, and updating them either to correct glaring flaws in the narrative or give better detail and setting for the eras when I wrote them.

Road Trip To Vegas: This is not in any chronological order right now, so this isn't something I started before works like *All Others Pay Cash* or *Snipe Hunt*. This is, however, based on an incident that happened long before I started my writing projects in earnest with my creative writing class in college. My family tends to drive to places, even long-distance, and so going on a road trip with my father was something that happened often in my teen years. There was in particular one trip – an emergency drive in December from Tampa Bay to

AUTHOR'S NOTES

Annapolis MD to rescue my older brother and his broken-down car – that left some lasting emotional scars on me, enough to create this story (and one other, a more supernatural tale directly based on that one road trip through the Virginia Tidewater region late at night in December).

My dad also inspired the trip being to Las Vegas: He was a Navy pilot for twenty years, and one of his duties was ferrying planes from coast-to-coast, meaning he and his flight group had various opportunities to visit Vegas during the early days of being a gambling oasis and not much else. Dad talked often and fondly about those trips, so I decided to make that into the story, told from my perspective. The more fantastical elements are of course pure fantasy. People really don't get the urge to plan a casino heist their first time visiting Vegas, after all. Right? (long pause) RIGHT?

I had written this story originally in 2011, tweaking and editing it over the years. I submitted it years later as an unpublished story for the Florida Writers Association's Royal Palm Literary Awards to see what the professional consensus would be. The judges kind of liked it, but it never got past the Semifinalist stage. One judge wrote back that they wanted to know more about the Yakuza boss nicknamed "Zero Cuts," feeling that was just a throw-away character deserving more love. Hmm. I could write a Zero Cuts story of him planning a casino heist... HEY WAIT A MINUTE, let's not go there. I could get in trouble with the casinos before I even get to Vegas.

All Others Pay Cash: This story came during the part of my life where I had just finished college, gotten a Master's degree in Library and Information Sciences, and started my first full-time job in South Florida in the Broward County system.

The origins of this story come both from the annual tax form overload that swamps the library system from January to April, and from a true-life incident where a woman dressed up as an angel came up to the reference desk at North Regional (Coconut Creek, FL) asking for tax forms. The woman actually was a 'Safety Angel,'

AUTHOR'S NOTES

performing for the children in the Youth Services area of the library that day. Three librarians, myself included, were sitting there at the desk, and all three of us had to look at those wings and had to be thinking 'Oh man, the IRS is really going after EVERYONE this time!' Well, anyway, I was thinking that.

The story was written for the annual writing contest held by *Writer's Digest*, one of the major creative writing services I could find at the time. I like writing contests: they force you to work within a deadline, and I can be notorious when it comes to suffering writer's block (there are fanfic readers for the *X-Files* still waiting for TWO works in progress to be done. Sorry, guys).

I thought this one stood a chance in the Short Story division, a lot better than the science fiction ones I had been submitting years earlier; however, this one still didn't get listed in the honorable mentions. Phooey on *Writer's Digest*: what do I have to do to impress you guys anyway?

By the by, this story became dated in the early 2000s when the spread of Adobe Reader and PDF formatting reduced the need for print copies of IRS forms. The spread of tax prep software also dwindled the demand. By 2012, only the basic forms were getting shipped to libraries. As of 2023, there's talk of the IRS setting up their own prep software to allow direct filing – something that's driving the tax help industry to suicide – to where libraries won't get tax forms and angels asking for them anymore.

Sunset View: I had originally titled this story "Dysiliou View," however Dysiliou is not a real word. It's a merging of the Greek translation for 'sunset', *Dys iliou*. At least I think it was, based on the English-to-Greek dictionaries. Problem is, the usage might be wrong. I know, there are a lot of Greek linguists who are plotting to sue me for emotional distress any minute now.

The island Dysiliou Key is not a real location, but I wanted to create a fictional locale in my hometown region of Tarpon Springs

AUTHOR'S NOTES

FL, some place, a fantasy spot of relaxation, that could be enjoyed, at least in my own head.

This story was written for a publication called *Glimmer Train*, which held writing contests almost every other month in poetry, short fiction, and general fiction. This didn't win in the category I submitted to, so well. This has been slightly revised with a few additional words towards the end, giving my two leads a little more material to work with. Casper Weinberger appears as an unpaid cameo: Also, I think he would claim he wasn't really in that photo anyway, so we'll cut him some slack on this one.

Fifth Annual Office Golf Showdown: This one is my prize winner. It received Second Place in 2002 with the Writers Network of South Florida, a group in the Broward/Palm Beach/Dade county region. Hi, everybody!

The inspiration for this story came from reading an article here, a book review there, about a growing new sport of, take a guess, office golf. Played like putt-putt, except in the offices of major corporations, and using the many floors within the skyscrapers these corporations are housed. One of the rules is that you've got to do it during actual work hours, when the Boss expects you to be earning your not-adjusted-for-costs-of-living minimum wage. I think one of the other rules is that when you're caught you're supposed to run for your life, but I could never confirm if anyone survived such moments.

The building used for this office golf story was based on any of the tall structures across the street from the Broward County Main Library in downtown Ft. Lauderdale, which you see every day from the staff lounge. I have never been inside any of those buildings, so the story relied a lot on speculation and hearsay.

When writing the story, I realized the best way to do it was through descriptions offered by running commentary, so I dragged in those media darlings the sports commentators. I also realized the story worked best sticking to dialogue, back-and-forth between the co-narrators. There was one point in the story where I realized the lack

AUTHOR'S NOTES

of dialogue, with one very short written sentence, could be funnier than anything spoken by a character, and I decided to make that the one point in the whole story where that happens for the best possible effect.

Personally, I took an adult vocational class on golf once, and took a couple of lessons to learn that I ought to stick to bowling.

Overdue: once more, into the breach dear friends once more. Yet another short story submitted to a *Writer's Digest* annual contest. Sigh. Are the submissions even getting to Cincinnati (from here on in, I'm paying the extra money to have the envelopes signed in when they get there)?

Librarianship can be a satisfying profession, and it is for me; however, you can run into some real stressful situations. One of the worst, at least for me, is when you have to deal with missing books, missing pages, missing anything. It gets frustrating for the people looking for something only to find some other jerk has walked off with it; and it turn it gets frustrating for the librarian doing his/her best to find these things for people.

I hate book thieves. I still haven't forgiven David Duchovny for the Torn Page Incident from the *X-Files* episode 'The Unnatural.' Do you hear me, David? Use the damn photocopier next time! Grr.

A magazine covering the library profession, *American Libraries*, published a humorous article I wrote on the various ways of stopping book thieves all the way back in February 2000, but in most respects I was utterly serious and in a bad mood when I wrote that list. I needed to work that frustration out of my system. One of the items on the list was that libraries should hire an elite ninja team to hunt down book thieves, which provided the basis for this story.

The character Warren Stern came from an earlier librarian story, in which he sets off to find the mythic Book With the Blue Cover (the incident is mentioned in passing here). The physical description from that early tale is mostly different from the one given here. Also, when I wrote this story I was still working with Broward Libraries: When I

AUTHOR'S NOTES

published this in my short story anthology by 2003, I had earned a job at Gainesville with the University of Florida, so I was a little worried they would prefer not being mentioned in a story like this. But I called over to UF Special Collections and they said it was okay to use their locale in the story, as long as I don't have any rogue FBI agents tearing out pages from their books (see, David? You've enraged more librarians than you can have possibly imagined). Chiyoko is brand new, inspired by the idealized vision of a female warrior. I've never been to Gonzaga but I'm a fan of their basketball program since the early 1990s, so I sent her there.

Troy Viator actually has appeared elsewhere in stories I'd written, in a younger version and as a doppelganger of sorts: he's me in fictional form (albeit working on a better diet: he's thinner than I'll ever be and looks cooler in a trench coat).

There's also a cameo by a real-life Rogue Librarian, although I've altered her name in the story to protect her true identity. I used to go by the nom de plume of Rogue Librarian on the Internet, but I found out she had gotten to that name before I did. I joke about her beating me in arm wrestling for it, and why not, she probably could too. I hope she doesn't mind that I have her humming the Spider-Man theme (from the 60s cartoon show). That should be a bit of a tip about this story: it's all basically a desperate attempt at a graphic novel with simplistic character motives and cheap stunts. But hey, if anyone wants to shop it around Hollywood, I'm listening!

Snipe Hunt: I write stories one of two ways; either I come up with a great opening line or I envision a nice ending that wraps up an unspecified event.

This one had a decent opening line that had been bugging me for years: 'Despite what people know, it does get cold in Florida.' I just like that opener. Unfortunately, I couldn't find a story to fit to it. For a while I was thinking of using it to describe a character coming back home for Christmas and dealing with a suicidal old friend, but

AUTHOR'S NOTES

honestly that's just too depressing to write. I wanted something with a little more wit and hope attached to it.

At some point I remembered an incident my older brother Eric told me from back in high school, where his marching band buddies dragged the freshmen at the summer band camp held in St. Leo out for a snipe hunt. And yes, the snipe hunt is a prank. But no, I'm not ruining it for anyone. Fer crying out loud, remember the gang on the *Cheers* show pulled this prank on Frasier? Even HE knew what it was. As long as it was harmless, it sounded like a fun little event. So I imagined a scenario where it wasn't done for fun but for a dark sadistic purpose. I realized holding a snipe hunt in the dead of winter, even in Florida, involved an introduction mentioning how cold it could get. I finally had a story to go with that line.

As I wrote the story, various things kept popping up for me to use. I wanted a cold front for clear skies, and also a full moon to give my protagonists some help in wandering the citrus grove. Having already established this early in the story as being on a Friday in January, I found the date of Jan. 17th fitting nicely. There was a full moon, there was a cold front blowing through at that time, and it was the Friday before the Tampa Bay Bucs football team went to Philadelphia to play the Eagles to get to that year's Super Bowl. So I had a character hoping to live long enough to see the team lose that Sunday, because at the time nobody believed the Bucs could win in cold weather against an Eagles team destined for the Super Bowl. In real life, that Sunday was one of Tampa Bay's biggest victories, with cornerback Ronde Barber icing the win with a 92-yard interception for a touchdown: To have a character foreshadow an ironic historical moment was a nice touch to keep in.

The story kept growing as I wrote it, and I know I went off on a few tangents in the telling of this tale. However, I like all of the bits that I've thrown in to the story, and can't really see myself parting with any of it. I'm not even sure if I'm ending it on the right note, and I've probably forced things a bit with Liam's final three thoughts. One

AUTHOR'S NOTES

thing as a writer, there's always an urge to add a little more, tweak a little more.

When I wrote this story in 2003, I hoped to work with these characters again, feeling I had created a nice set of characters and history. Alas, as I've grown older I've moved away from how these characters could continue their stories, and I admit I've abandoned them to their fates somewhere in the morass of Florida suburbia. This is 20 years later. I miss them.

The Spanish translations were provided by co-workers at University of Florida, taking the original lines generated from an online website and correcting all the grammar errors that cropped up. They were from Guatemala and so the Spanish will reflect that regional dialect, but hopefully it fits into the migrant patterns here in Florida.

Welcome To Florida: I began writing this story in 2010, finishing it up by 2011 during which I was intrigued by the then-new development in direct publishing for eBooks via Amazon for their Kindle readers and Barnes and Noble for their Nook readers. So instead of going through the struggles of submitting to publishers, I decided to publish this as an eStory.

When I wrote this, the movement to decriminalize pot usage for medicinal purposes was a major development in Florida (and most of the nation). I am not a pot-user myself – I don't even drink alcohol, I tend to be insanely sober – but I've read on the topic and for what I knew then (and now) was that the benefits outweighed the risks. As long as we regulated cannabis and its chemical off-shoots the way we regulate beer and cigarettes, I didn't really see the harm of it. So I wrote this story with an eye on throwing in the memetic craziness of the state of Florida itself. The stuff about the alligators are a little exaggerated – they can't climb through windows, so you're safe – but they do get frisky during mating season, so be careful at the water margins okay?

I was also writing this story during a bad bout of unemployment, having moved from UF to Pasco County Libraries in 2006 but losing

AUTHOR'S NOTES

that job by 2008. I just wasn't a good fit there. But I lost work at the start of the Great Recession, which tightened the job market not only with my field of work but across most of the state. So in-between looking for full-time work and even part-time work to help pay the bills between 2009 to 2013, I tried writing stories to get direct-published. And well, without high-end marketing, you're not going to sell a lot of stories by yourself. Sigh.

Where the Snow Is Gray: This originated from a team project started with the Writers 4 All Seasons critique group back in 2015 or so. Ostensibly a project to teach fellow writers about deadlines, the editorial process, and the overall publication process, it saw a brief moment of actual publication as an anthology *Stories For All Seasons* (guess the theme!) on Kindle as an eBook. However, the group's struggle to organize for tax purposes and to set up a bank account to manage any revenues from the sales fell apart, and the anthology got pulled from market.

I had asked the remaining group leadership about the possibility of retaking the story so I could get it published myself, and there were no arguments against it as it was my story and there's no discernable copyright issue involved (I hope). So here it is.

I had originally envisioned this story as being part of another "universe" I was working with at the time, a superhero-themed setting with the character Jenny going through her superhero origin during the early drafts. For the purposes of the seasonal theme of the anthology, I removed the fantasy/superhero elements and stuck with the Coming Of Age elements of Jenny coping with a dysfunctional family.

The title of the story comes from a mondegreen of me mishearing the opening lyrics to Tori Amos' song "Winter." Person-ally, I've never coped with snow in my lifetime. When my family lived in Virginia Beach for a few years – the furthest north I've ever lived – we didn't get snow, it was more of a slush. Never more than an inch, and never enough to build a snowman. Yes, I have regrets.

AUTHOR'S NOTES

So I have no idea if I've used snow in the proper context here. My apologies.

The Hide and Seek Suitcase: This story has its origins from a writing prompt given at a critique meeting of the Lakeland Writers group, sometime around 2015 or so. The early form of this was done in a ten-minute rush on the prompt "What would you find in your suitcase?" From that I created a quick story about my character finding a stolen object taken during a questionably unethical drinking binge with an unscrupulous family member. I recall the other writers attending that they were amused by the backstory I was able to suggest with the final lines of text.

A few years later – was it 2017? – the statewide Florida Writers Association held their annual anthology contest with a theme of mystery. I remembered this little snippet, dug it out, and expanded on the background some more to help fit the anthology's theme.

The submission didn't make the cut. Ah well.

The story is NOT autobiographical, okay? For starters, I don't drink. Besides, I'm not confessing to anything and my alibis are solid.

That Last Minute Thing: This story began as a follow-up story project with Writers 4 All Season, where we were planning to interconnect stories based on a location – this time, a fictional knock-off of Wal-Mart – with our characters intermingling and overlapping each other's stories. As you're reading this story, you can see various side-line characters getting set up: The door greeter for example was someone one of the other writers had created for her story, and I was setting up the wandering dog, the half-naked woman, and wheel-chair-bound customer for other writers to pick up. This project fell apart as the publication woes of the first project nearly split the writing group, and so this story remained untold until now.

You may notice the story written in fragment sentences most of the time. I was attempting to convey the half-awake internal dialogue of the narrating character, where the thoughts came half-formed and

AUTHOR'S NOTES

barely following any rationale. When the project was unfinished by 2016, the ending for the story wasn't even on paper, so when I dusted this off for inclusion here I worked on that, creating several twists until I decided on the one I went with here. It fit the mood I was in back in those years, especially my desire to get a Lego Millennium Falcon set. I was in my late 40s at the time and people had stopped buying me toys for birthdays. Sigh. This hit me with a vengeance by 2022 though, when my family found out I was still into Lego and then all of a sudden I had five Star Wars sets I couldn't possibly work on. (I've run out of shelf space to display them, alas)

Just Throwing This Out There: Half of what I'm publishing in this anthology comes from writing prompts and anthology requests. This is mostly due to the other story projects I'm working on being more large-scale, and intended for bigger things. I'm just including these so you all can see where my mind takes me when I write.

This story came from one of those writing prompts where the moderator shares a number of generic-seeming photos and getting you to write about one (or more) image inspiring you. If I recall, this was from a Writers 4 All Seasons prompt where one of the photos was a dark forest and another photo was a happy large puppy. Where the scorpion came from, well, that was from a personal incident at a high school Christmas party my senior year. Yes, I am still traumatized by that.

I worked with all dialogue again, seeing as this was a quick writing prompt and as the story I had didn't need much description other than from the two characters' interactions. This might have been a fun flash fiction story to submit somewhere, but I just cannot figure at the moment how to expand out this story.

The original work, being a flash fiction writing prompt, didn't even have a title. I am just literally throwing this out there.

A Wandering Muse: Another story meant for the Florida Writers Association annual contest, that year's being "Where Does My Muse

AUTHOR'S NOTES

Reside?" My story's rough introduction started off with "Well, my muse resides in a travelogue, and she's not answering her phone." And the narrative evolved from there.

The idea was that the muse "comes to life" in the writer's mind, filling in plot and action scenes at all the various places he visits during his vacation. The original draft was much shorter, given the word-count limitations of the contest. In this anthology, I have more room to flesh out the story with more detail and more exploding cars.

As mentioned, I submitted this to FWA. It didn't get accepted.

I like writing contests because they give me focus. I hate rejections because they give me frustration. Sigh.

Last Prayer: I am a sucker for the occasional weird submission requests that the literary marketplace throws out there from time to time. This came about when I saw a submission request for stories based on Bruce Springsteen songs. Having been a fan since the early 1980s, and especially a huge fan of the song "Open All Night" from the album *Nebraska*, I typed out this story in short order and submitted it for consideration.

It didn't get selected.

Most writers will tell you rejection letters happen all the time (the rest will sit in silence with gentle tears rolling down their cheeks as they stir their coffee). It's a frustrating process. There's a reason why these stories are showing up in this collection and not in the *New Yorker*. Or a hundred other magazines or anthologies.

I also get the feeling the editors were more fans of the album *Wrecking Ball*. Curses.

The Voynich Key: This story started as a submission for an anthology prompt I found online via the *Submission Grinder* website. A fantasy/science fiction publisher wanted to put together an anthology based on a theme, with a shared protagonist character called "The Librarian" moving through time and space performing heroic bibliographic deeds.

AUTHOR'S NOTES

As a librarian who wants to write in that science fiction genre, I was intrigued, and I got working on a project that had been in my head ever since I heard about the real-life Voynich Manuscript (Yes, it is real and safely stored so that no rogue wizards can pilfer it). The story idea originally involved the characters from my earlier work *Overdue*, which is why you see Viator returning here and the others mentioned in passing.

When I finished the rough draft, I still had about two weeks before deadline to get it critiqued by my writing groups, who helped flesh out some of the details and got the story more streamlined. I got to a more polished draft a few days before deadline.

And then I stared at the story and suddenly didn't like it. Something about it was still off, something felt forced. The ending, I realized, didn't really end on a proper resolution, it just had the villain discouraged from stealing the second Voynich book and walking away. I couldn't change anything about it because when I tried to add a better ending the story went over the required word-count limit.

So I ended up not submitting it to that contest. It's a regret, but at the time it wasn't a good story to offer to them, and I admit that.

With this anthology, with the room I have to expand upon the work, I was able to add the ending I wanted and that I feel works better. I did have to go back in and revise the character's origins and purpose, since I could no longer have her as the "Librarian" of that anthology, and had to make herself her own. Some of the details from that work still leaked through.

As for the situation with Waldo, FL being a world-famous speed trap, that actually ended by 2018 when the town's police force was disbanded and taken over by the county sheriff's office. It's still not recommended to go speeding through there. As a result, this does date this story as happening by 2017 at the latest.

The Girl With Angel Wings: Yet again a story meant for a contest submission, this one also for the Florida Writers Association's annual anthology. The theme for this contest was "Secrets," and I

AUTHOR'S NOTES

had in mind a story idea about a woman discovering her husband having an affair, and enduring a complex confrontation with the mistress who didn't realize she was talking to the scorned wife.

I admit I am not an expert on relationships, however the narrative appeal of having two characters interacting where one was clueless about the harm being done was strong, and having her be a nice girl at heart – even trying to console the woman she'd unintentionally broken – be the twist to make the story fresh (at least in my mind).

When I read this to the Writers 4 All Seasons group, they loved that twist, and liked the two characters anchoring the short story. They talked me into cutting out some extraneous details and it helped improve the flow of the story, and that I sent in for consideration.

It didn't get accepted.

I know these contests are contests for a reason, that not every submission survives the judging process. I know I'm going up against hundreds of other writers in my state, and that a lot of them are getting the rejections as well.

It's just, at some point you want to clear that hurdle, get an acceptance, feel like the years of typing away reached some achievement. I've gotten awards for my non-fiction blogging, which is great, I've felt inspired about keeping that going as part of my writing interests. It's just... I'd like to think I'm good at this fiction stuff as well. When I've gotten some of my humor/horror stories accepted by the *Strangely Funny* anthologies over the years, those were always helpful keeping my drive to write going. But all the rejections in all the other stuff I try to write – the humor stuff, the straight science fiction stories, the supernatural road-trip story I really think is some of my best writing that I've submitted to at least eight different publishers by now, even a story or two in the mystery genre – just hits the soul pretty hard.

This is where I am, spiritually, in my writing interests. There's still a lot of projects in my head and on my flash drive that I hope to finish, especially the superhero stories I've been working on the past (checks notes) fifteen years or more. Sigh.

AUTHOR'S NOTES

I've been told often that the reader you need to impress is yourself, try to enjoy and accept your own writing. Thing is, we're still crafting this literary art for you all to read and enjoy as well.

I hope I can get better at this.

Paul Wartenberg
October 29, 2023

ABOUT THE AUTHOR

Paul Wartenberg is a professional reference librarian, a semi-professional political blogger, a semi-literate writer with various short stories published over the years, and a long-time resident of Florida who knows he's too crazy to live elsewhere (anything north of I-10 is frozen wasteland!!!) but too sober to handle it.

Paul reads a large number of comic books, watches a lot of science fiction, plays a little too much *Pokemon Go* for his own good, and is just starting to get into *Magic: The Gathering* card gaming. You might remember him from many years of playing *City of Heroes* MMO, and writing *X-Files* fanfic and 'Shipper surveys involving Mulder and Scully.

Paul has been published in other anthology collections such as the *Strangely Funny* series, *Mardi Gras Murder*, and *History & Mystery Oh My*.

He is owned by two cats.

Official website at https://paulwstories.com/

Book cover by M A Rehman

Made in the USA
Columbia, SC
21 January 2024